BALDUR'S SONG

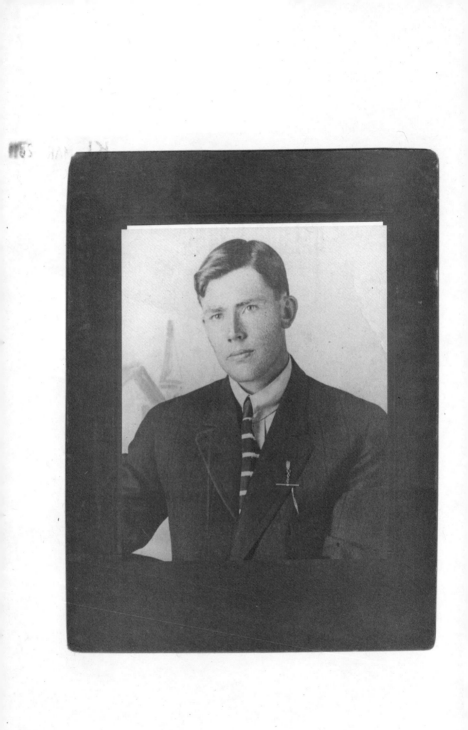

BALDUR'S SONG: A SAGA

by

David Arnason

TURNSTONE PRESS

Turnstone Press
Artspace Building
206-100 Arthur Street
Winnipeg, MB
R3B 1H3 Canada
www.TurnstonePress.com

Turnstone Press gratefully acknowledges the assistance of the Canada Council for the Arts, the Manitoba Arts Council, the Government of Canada through the Canada Book Fund, and the Province of Manitoba through the Book Publishing Tax Credit and the Book Publisher Marketing Assistance Program.

Portions of this novel first appeared in slightly different form in *Prairie Fire* magazine.

Cover design: Jamis Paulson
Interior design: Sharon Caseburg
Printed and bound in Canada by Friesens for Turnstone Press.

Photos in this book appear courtesy David Arnason and the Archives of Manitoba. A full list of photo credits appear on page 237.

Library and Archives Canada Cataloguing in Publication

Arnason, David, 1940-
    Baldur's song / David Arnason.

ISBN 978-0-88801-373-6

    1. Winnipeg (Man.)--Fiction. I. Title.

PS8551.R765B36 2010   C813'.54   C2010-902281-5

Mixed Sources
Cert no. SW-COC-001271
© 1996 FSC
FSC

For Mhari

BALDUR'S SONG

I was born at the beginning of the Second World War. That was not my intention. The signs were all wrong. There was too much violence, too much bad feeling and the weather was terrible. I would have liked to have been born a decade later, and I did what I could to resist any entry to this world, but that was not to be. I refused to leave my mother's body, until the doctor took a pair of forceps and hauled me, unwilling and screaming, into the operating room at the Johnson Memorial Hospital in Gimli. The first thing I saw was nuns in black-and-white habits, fluttering about like inadequate birds of prey, and I was terrified of them. I am still terrified of nuns, though these days it is more difficult to identify them.

It was Thursday night and the worst thunderstorm of the season was raging. My father later told me that it was hard to know whether the storm or my baby self was the louder. I suppose I should be grateful that the bombs that were dropping in Europe on my fellow babies were absent in Manitoba, but I was in no mood to be grateful at the time.

My first perception was that I was entirely powerful, and the world was waiting for me. I was sure that, with the exception of the flapping nuns, I was the only person of consequence in the world. I soon learned there were others. My father was from a family of ten and my mother from a family of eleven, and they were all busy replicating themselves and filling the Canadian prairies with my cousins. Still, I clung to the notion of my special nature. I was sure I would not have been ripped from mother's womb and sent into this world unless destiny had plans for me.

And of course it did, but before I tell you about that, I have to pay homage to my ancestors who suffered mightily to bring me to this place. I cannot tell you my story until they have had their proper due. I will begin with the charmed moments when my ancestors made their decision to move to the new world. They left Iceland not with the intention of becoming Canadians or even Americans, but with the hope of creating a New Iceland in the new world.

And so I begin with a prelude to America, and the story of my great-great-grandmother Petrina Soffia Arngrimsdottir. In fact, I will go back further and invoke her mother Thorunn and her father Arngrimur to begin my tale.

PRELUDE TO AMERICA

She shouldn't have done it. She shouldn't have lain with him there in the sweet meadow, the sun low in the sky, the music still ringing in her ears. So what if he had played on the violin while everyone danced, so what if he sang like an angel? She was only seventeen and he was the father of five children, so what if her blood had flooded her body like a disease, she should have said no, I can find my own way home, thank you. She should have said I am sorry, sir, what you ask is impossible. The nineteenth century had tipped on its fulcrum and they were sliding towards a new century, but there was still plenty of time. She could have said no.

But she didn't. It's a curse on the whole family. We can't say no. When somebody invites us to pleasure, we forget what we were doing, we forget all our plans, and we're thrashing in the bedclothes or crushing the flowers in the sweet meadows. There was plenty of warning. The gulls were crying out danger, the terns were calling beware, beware. The heat of the blood is no excuse, but we make it our excuse again and again.

And that's what Thorunn did in the Icelandic dawn when the century was gathering itself for disaster. She forgot she could recite whole sections of the Bible, that her father was the priest at Tjorn, that her mother had warned against such a moment. So this is love, she thought, and she slipped out of her dress as if it had no buttons, as if it had been designed to be thrown carelessly on the grass. Even the starlings were upset. They flew out over the fjord so that they would not have to watch, they flew right past the swans nesting near the mouth of the river, they flew north in the direction of the Arctic Circle, which hovered just on the edge of the horizon.

Ah, but when it was over she was sorry, you want to say, she had learned her lesson, but it was nothing of the sort. It's a curse on the whole family, this inability to feel proper guilt, to learn from our mistakes. We should be wearing sackcloth and ashes, some of us should learn how to pray properly, somebody should ask for forgiveness. But we don't. At least Thorunn didn't. She danced home as happily as if she had won first prize in the confirmation class.

And she did it again. The very next night. She slipped out of doors when she should have been sleeping and lay with Arngrimur again, just beyond the church in plain view of her father's bedroom, in plain view of her own grandmother's grave. And the next day, when she should have stayed in her room and begged the Lord's forgiveness, she told her sister everything, she told Petrina Soffia who was only fifteen how love happens, the mechanics of the thing. She said it all aloud in the barn when they were feeding the new calf, when anyone might have been listening.

It's a curse on the whole family. We can't keep anything to ourselves. We have to blab it all out, to tell each other things that should never be spoken aloud. We have no secrets, none of us, and no shame. Don't tell us anything, we will tell everyone else, we don't even whisper. You may as well publish your secret in the newspaper as tell it to us.

And so by the end of the week everyone in the valley knew.

Thorunn was so happy about being in love and so amazed with the simple dynamics of lovemaking she told everything to Petrina Soffia. And Petrina was so amazed at her sister's discovery that she told Nanna and Inga, and even their little brother Bjorn, who was only five years old. And Nanna told Disa and Inga told Margaret, and Bjorn who didn't understand asked Thorunn, who kissed him and said not to worry, everything would be fine.

That's another problem. We all believe that everything can be cured with kisses. There's no use telling us kisses are part of the problem, that kisses might be the whole problem. We kiss each other when we meet and we kiss each other when we part, and we sometimes kiss perfect strangers. I'll tell you more about that later.

And of course everybody in the valley knew in no time. This is a valley that can't keep secrets. Secrets slide down the slopes of the mountains. Elves whisper the secrets to the cattle. The wind from the fjord blows nobody any good.

So by the time that Arngrimur's wife found out, Thorunn's belly had begun to swell. The swans on the pond kept their dignity. They nodded their heads and looked at their reflections in the water. The glacier in the south end of the valley moved one more notch toward the fjord. Half the people in the valley packed their bags and moved to America. Arngrimur bowed his head like a swan and stayed in his house.

Thorunn looked at her reflection in the water and she liked what she saw, the rounding of her belly. She was without shame. When Arngrimur walked by on the road she waved to him, and she laughed a laugh that haunted him for nine years. He woke in the night in his bed, and the laugh rattled him so he couldn't sleep, and he had to get up in the dark and breathe deeply one hundred times before he could sleep again. For nine whole years.

Did I tell you that we're all plagued by ghosts? Every last one of us, even here in America. It's like this. There were so many ghosts in the valley, there wasn't room for them. And so many people left for

America, there was nobody left for the ghosts, so they went to America too, though not until 1883. One of them is always after me to move his bones. But that comes later. Remind me to tell you about it.

So while Arngrimur was dealing with that ghost of a laugh, Thorunn's father was making arrangements. He could have sent her to America, but she didn't want to go, and he thought she might get into even more trouble there, in a place that wasn't an island, so you could go anywhere you wanted. And so he married her off to Jon Helgason.

Actually, it wasn't so easy. She didn't want to marry Jon Helgason, even though he had his own farm down the valley, just at the foot of the glacier where the river makes a turn and the bridge keeps falling down. Even though his wife had been dead for ten years, and even though he had his own house and his own sheep and he promised she could have her own horse. Even then she resisted. But then her brother Bjorn drowned in the pond, and everything was too much for a while, and when things settled she was married and had a daughter.

It was a time when children often died, and Thorunn's daughter died too, even though Thorunn did everything she could to keep her alive. It was the whooping cough that took her in the middle of the night, and none of Thorunn's prayers moved God to intervene. Arngrimur was in sorrow too, though he couldn't show it. When Thorunn cried at the funeral, her cry entered Arngrimur's soul, and it haunted him for nine years. Every morning when he awoke, he was so sad he had to take one hundred deep breaths before he could get out of his bed.

Jon Helgason was old, there's no denying that. He was sixty-six when he married Thorunn, and they were married for four years before she shared his bed. Perhaps she was waiting for Arngrimur, but after a while, there seemed no point in waiting. She had to make the best of things. That's a good thing about us. We all make the best of things. Life isn't always fair, and you have to take what you are given.

Thorunn had two sons with Jon, but they were both albinos with white hair and pink eyes. Jon was so old that his seed had gone bad, and it wasn't strong enough to make a child who could live. Both boys died at the age of two, and Thorunn decided she would have no more children.

But then Arngrimur's wife died, and he was left alone. His oldest daughter Nanna moved off to America, and the younger children went to live with other people, so he was all by himself. He decided to live his life as a hermit, but he was the only one in the valley who could play the violin, and he was the only one in the valley who could play the flute, and the people needed music, and so even though he was unhappy, he sang and he played, and even though he yearned for Thorunn, and woke in the night to her laugh and in the morning to her cry, he was caught by his life and he had to live it.

And so after a wedding where he had played and sung, he lay in the sweet meadow with another young woman. Only once, he swore, and only half-willingly, because she had asked him to. It's a curse on the whole family. We are too polite to refuse, and so rather than hurt anyone's feelings, we populate the planet with the fruits of accidental love. Arngrimur found himself the father of another daughter. I don't know what became of that daughter. I ought to know. It's written in a book, and I could look it up, but I don't want to. That's a different story, not the story I want to tell.

Here's what happened next. Jon Helgason was climbing onto the back of a horse. He put one foot in the stirrup and swung his leg over the horse. Only he didn't stop. He continued right over the horse onto the ground on the other side, and when Thorunn came to help him up, he was dead.

They buried him right there on the farm, in the exact spot where he had died. And the grass had not even started to grow on his grave before Thorunn married Arngrimur. Nobody in the valley spoke ill of them for that. Everyone knew they had been meant for each other from the start, and only bad luck had kept them apart. The day they married was nine years after Arngrimur had heard Thorunn's laugh and his haunting had begun. She laughed again, the night of their wedding, and after that, Arngrimur slept through the night. She cried the next morning for all of their lost children, and Arngrimur never heard her cry again.

The twentieth century was coming at them like an avalanche and they didn't have much time. They set to work and had four more children. The whole family is like that. When something needs to be done, we get right down to it and do it. Nobody in the valley was happier than Arngrimur and Thorunn. Once, the new priest preached a sermon which everybody knew was aimed at them. It told a parable about the dangers of lying in the sweet meadows with people who you should not be lying with, but Arngrimur and Thorunn were so happy that the story ended up with the wrong moral, and the priest never preached it again.

Their children were Nanna and Bjorn and Angantyr and Petrina Soffia, every one of them named for someone else, because that's one way of keeping the dead alive. And after a while Arngrimur died. I don't like to talk about his death, but I have a long story to tell and it's best to get the hard parts done early. It was pneumonia. He forgot his coat and walked home without it. A sudden storm brought sleet and rain off the ocean, and Arngrimur caught pneumonia and died.

So this is where the real story begins, after Arngrimur's death when the family had to go and live with relatives and there were twenty-two people living in one house. The story is about the second Petrina Soffia, daughter of Thorunn and Arngrimur, who was beautiful and good and looked so much like her mother the people in the valley had trouble telling the difference. On her seventeenth birthday, an old farmer down the valley, a nephew of Jon Helgason, offered to marry Petrina Soffia. I told you there were twenty-two people living in the house, so it was hard for her to refuse.

Petrina Soffia asked her mother what she should do.

Thorunn said only one word.

"America."

And so Petrina Soffia packed up everything she owned, all her clothes and her books, and she put them in her suitcase and she walked all the way to the harbour and boarded a boat and sailed for America. Nobody in Iceland ever heard from her again.

She brought more than her clothes and her books. She brought a memory of mountains and glaciers and fjords. She brought the taste of wild berries on mountain slopes and she carried in her lungs the freshest air in the world. She brought a thousand songs her father had taught her and she brought the memory of how to make pönnukökur and *skyr* and how to knit sweaters and how to keep a dying lamb alive. She gathered up all the lonely and abandoned ghosts in Iceland and brought them with her. She brought sweet meadows and the cry of gulls.

And when the boat finally landed in Quebec, she stepped right off into America and into the twentieth century and she never looked back.

Lucky for us.

And of course it was lucky for us. Petrina Soffia died in childbirth at the age of twenty. Her daughter, my grandmother, Petrina Thorunn Soffia Anderson, inherited her mother's spirit and her grandmother's spirit, and she brought an enormous family into being before she died at the age of ninety-nine. We numbered one hundred and fifty-seven at last count, and even now more are awaiting their entrance into this world.

Mothers are important, but they are not the only story. My grandfather's father, Johann Arnason known as Johann Sterkur, Johann the Strong, had his own story to tell. He was a free thinker in an age when religion was powerful, and he often found himself in problems because of his views. Free thinkers are not much more popular today than they were then, but the free thinking that Johann brought with him to Canada was so powerful that it affects the whole family still.

Family gatherings can only agree on a few things. The government is corrupt and its leaders should be horsewhipped. No use to tell us that horsewhipping has gone out of style along with the horses that presumably got the whipping. Horsewhipping it is. The weather is getting worse every year. The present concerns about global warming stand us in good stead. We have been warning our friends about the weather for over a hundred years. Finally, we all agree that what passes for morality in this world is the hypocrisy of those with special interests who want to foist their beliefs on others so that they can profit. These shared beliefs bring a certain harmony to our gatherings, but they often cause disturbances when people other than the family are gathered. On the other hand, the family is so large that there is little need to spend time with other people. We have all the variety that we need. Granted, we must marry outside the family, but those we marry tend to get absorbed so thoroughly they forget they were not born into it.

But back to Johann, a giant of a man. When I was a child there were still people who could recite his story, and in the remote and icy regions of Villingadal, the remotest farm in the remotest region of Iceland, there are still some who claim to have known him. People live a long time there, and memories are passed from generation to generation, as if they were still fresh.

THERE WERE GIANTS, THEN

The nineteenth century was ending. Everybody was going to America. Europe had convulsed and a tide of human bodies rocked their way across the Atlantic. The twentieth century loomed just beyond the horizon, and those who listened carefully could hear its beat, a sort of low intimation of jazz. Everybody was dressing in blue those days. It was a time for wearing blue.

Arni Petursson was not going to America. America was a place for madmen and fools. He didn't believe in America. When the talk turned to America he started to talk about sheep. He wouldn't listen to any nonsense about ships and rich farmland and opportunities. He would talk about horses instead.

Villingadal is the highest farm in the whole valley. Beyond Villingadal is only lava and snow. The river begins in Villingadal, a spring in the side of the mountain, and by the time it reaches the fjord, it is too wide to cross. "What business do Icelanders have in America?" Arni asked anyone who would listen. "Aren't there enough sheep and horses in Iceland without roaming the whole world?"

There's a strain of that in the family, a kind of crankiness that won't let us believe anything we haven't seen with our own eyes. Sometimes it can keep you out of trouble, but it can also get you into fights. We're fighters, that's for sure.

The problem was that the bull had gone to America with Thorgeir and his family, and since he had gone, the ice had frozen in the fjord, and for three years in a row there was no summer. The sky filled with ash and darkened, and no grass grew. The sheep died in the fields, and the horses died in the mountains, and the people went to America, and even the ghosts went with them.

Thorgeir's Bull had vowed to haunt Thorgeir's family for nine generations, just because Thorgeir's grandfather, Thorgeir the Bald, had given him an indignity. That Thorgeir had gone in to have supper when the bull was only half-skinned after he had killed it. It was a stupid thing to do. Anyone knows that if you don't finish skinning an animal it will come back and haunt you.

And now Thorgeir Thorgeirsson, son of Thorgeir Thorgeirsson the Bald, son of Thorgeir Thorgeirsson the Strong, had gone to America and the bull had gone with him. The bull had been a nuisance, trampling the rhubarb at night, coming as a barking dog and frightening the sheep, bellowing in the high passes until finally the wind joined him in his howling, and storms made the river flood, even right there in the valley where it began. But the bull kept the other ghosts under control, and Arni missed it.

Did I tell you that on that side we are descended from giants? Arni Petursson was a full two yards in height and all of his sons and daughters were taller than him. They were the finest *glíma* wrestlers in all of Eyjafjordur. All four of the boys could beat anyone but his own brothers, and each of the three girls could beat any man in the district.

The famous Lifting Rock was right there in Villingadal, just south of the barn. Arni Petursson had lifted it, and his father, Petur Arnason, had lifted it as had his father Arni Petursson and so on back to the giants who had first put it there when the world began. All of the sons could lift the rock and so could all of the daughters, but there was no other man in the north of Iceland who could budge it. The girls had vowed they would marry no man who could not lift the rock, and so Margaret had to wait until Sveinn Bjornsson came from Reykjavik and lifted it, and Helga had to wait until Grimsi Magnusson came from the east and lifted it, and Disa would never have married at all if a Norwegian named Bjorn hadn't come and lifted it when Disa was forty years old, and nearly past child-bearing. But that's a different story. I'll tell it to you another time.

It's Johann I want to tell you about, and the courting of Dorothea Soffia Abrahamsdottir. Here's what happened. When Johann was seventeen years old, he went to a tombola at Grund on the other side of the river. His mother wanted to go, because her sister Rosa was going to be there, and Arni told Johann to take her, because there was haying to do, and the sun had finally come out after forty days of rain.

Johann did not want to go when there was work to be done, but he saddled up two horses and he and his mother rode for two hours along the path to the bridge across the river. Then they rode two hours back along the other side of the river until they came to Grund. The tombola was just as boring as Johann had thought it would be. But just as his mother was saying goodbye to her sister Rosa, Dorothea Soffia Abrahamsdottir walked into the room. She had long black hair and hazel eyes. Johann heard a loud crack, like the sound of thunder or the crack of an earthquake, and he realized it was his heart that had made the noise. Dorothea smiled at him, and he felt as if his insides had turned to liquid. Then he ran out of the room, harnessed the horses, and gathered up his mother to take her home.

It was too late. He was hooked so solidly into love that there was no chance that he could ever be free again. All the way to the bridge he cursed his fate, and swore that he would never be made a slave, but his heart was paying no attention to him. It had begun singing, and

Dorothea's image was imprinted on the inside of his eyelids, so that even if he closed his eyes, he still saw her.

Johann's mother told him to forget about her. Dorothea was the daughter of Abraham Hallgrimsson from Hlidihagi, the richest man in Eyjafordur and his wife Fridrika, who was famous for her beauty. She was descended from Norwegian kings. She would not marry Johann Arnason, the son of Arni Petursson who didn't even believe in America.

Johann agreed with his mother. He knew there was no chance in the world that Dorothea had even noticed him or even if she did notice him, that she would marry him. But that didn't stop him from dreaming of her all that night and all the next night too. It didn't stop him from thinking of her all day long and it didn't stop his heart from singing its own maddening song.

Then one week later, just at dusk, Johann looked up from the stones he was piling for a fence and he saw a figure in a black robe on the top of the cliff on the other side of the river. He knew immediately that it was Dorothea. Nobody had ever appeared at the edge of that cliff before, and Johann knew what it meant.

He ran to the stone bridge that crossed the river down by the waterfall. It was the only way across the river unless you harnessed a horse and rode for two hours. The trouble was that the cliff was twenty yards high, and it was perfectly vertical. There was barely a foothold anywhere, but that didn't bother Johann. He clambered up the cliff as if he were a goat. He forgot that he was two yards tall and he weighed two hundred twenty pounds and that he would be a certain corpse if he fell. It was pitch dark when he reached the top, and Dorothea was nowhere to be seen.

He shouted her name, but she did not answer. Then he caught a whiff of her perfume on the air, and he followed that smell for a mile until he came to a mighty farm with a dozen barns. The farmhouse had glass windows, something that Johann had heard about but had never seen before. Through the windows, the light of lamps poured out onto the ground, and inside, he could see a figure in a black robe.

He was looking through the window when the men of Hlidihagi jumped on him. Eight men grabbed him and struck at him. They called him a dog, and swore he would regret that he had come onto the land of his betters. It was a mighty battle but when it was over, Johann had stacked all eight of the men in a pile and knocked at the door. A man in rich clothes answered the door and asked him what he wanted. He said he wanted to speak with Dorothea, and gave his name.

"You are the son of Petur Arnason?"

"Yes."

"I am Abraham Hallgrimsson. Let me shake your hand."

Johann gave Abraham his hand, and Abraham squeezed his hand harder than any man had ever squeezed it before. Johann returned the squeeze, and the two men stood there locked together until finally Abraham relented and called Dorothea.

She was even more beautiful than he had remembered, and Johann suddenly felt himself gross and clumsy. His legs were the thickness of tree trunks, his chest like a barrel, his head a block of wood thatched with yellow straw, his eyes a no-colour blue, and she was delicate and dark.

"May I call on you?" he asked.

"You may come on Sunday," she said. "I will see you at the church."

"I will come Sunday at afternoon coffee," he told her. "I will not enter a church."

"You will not be welcome then," she said.

"We'll see," he answered, and he walked back out the door. The men had unstacked themselves, and were moaning and cursing, but they did not try their luck with Johann again.

Somehow, he climbed back down the cliff and made his way home. His father was waiting for him.

"Is it a sacrilege to enter a church if you do not believe?" Johann asked him.

"You may enter for weddings and funerals," his father said. "But if you enter for any other reason, then you are a hypocrite."

Johann said nothing, but he sat outside in the damp night for hours, pondering out what he must do. He could not marry a wife who would insist he go to church, and if he did not go to church, it appeared Dorothea would not be his wife.

The next night was Friday, but he scaled the cliff anyway and made his way to Abraham's farm. This time he did not go close, but only sat on a rock and watched the farm until dawn. Then he climbed back down the cliff and went home.

The third night he sat on the fence near one of the barns. The lights were out in the house, and Johann stared so hard in his desire to see Dorothea that he nearly lighted up the house by the heat of his gaze. Then without warning, his eyes were covered by soft hands, and a sweet voice whispered his name.

"Will you marry me?" he asked.

"Yes," she said. "I will marry you somehow, though it will have to be without my father's permission if you cannot go to church."

"I cannot do it."

"Then we'd better get busy," she said. "If we are going to marry without a church, then there is no need to wait. You may call me Soffia." And she led him to the barn, and there in the barn was the making of Fridrika Johannsdottir begun.

Afterwards, they walked together to the cliff.

"What do we do now?" Johann asked.

Soffia looked deep into his lake-blue eyes.

"America," she said, and she kissed him again.

Then the waves of the Atlantic began to fret, and storms hurried down from the north. All the birds in Iceland rose up in protest, and cried out their dismay. But the St. Lawrence River swelled and America opened its arms and prepared to receive them, and there was nothing left that anyone could do.

I met Dorothea once when I was a child and she was a very old lady. She was dressed in a long brown dress and her hair was tied up in a bun. My father had brought me to her house because he had some errand to do for his grandmother. She reached into her pocket and pulled out a peppermint. I remember the peppermint was brown from being in her pocket, but it was the sweetest thing I had ever tasted.

By that time, Johann was dead. He had homesteaded the farm called Espiholi, aspen hill, and begun his dynasty. He was a great chess player, an expert at the kind of Icelandic wrestling called *glíma* and a fisherman and a farmer. He had arrived with the big group of Icelandic settlers in 1883, and took part in the renaissance of New Iceland that began then. He had a sharp eye for ghosts and he claimed to know several of them personally. His son, my great-grandfather, Baldur Arnason, had little use for ghosts, but more of him later.

It was my mother's father who was the most familiar with spirits, however. My maternal grandfather, Thorstein Andress Anderson, was descended from wizards. His great-grandfather Tomas was a wizard near Akureyri in the north of Iceland. He had gotten into an argument about money with one of his neighbours and so he decided to send a spirit against him. He went with his son to the churchyard near his home and at the stroke of midnight, he made an incantation over one of the graves, and immediately a spirit came out of the ground. To make a spirit do your bidding, you have to kiss it full on the mouth and mix your saliva with the saliva of the dead. At the moment of the kiss, Tomas realized the corpse he had just raised was the corpse of his own father, and so he did not complete the kiss. The spirit then began to drag him into the grave. His son came running to help, but the spirit let go of Tomas and began to drag the boy into the grave. Tomas realized there was only one cure for this dilemma. He ran to the church and began to ring the church bell. The spirit lost all strength and returned to its grave. His son was terrified but alive. His father had planned to teach him how to be a wizard, but after that day he had no interest in wizardry.

My grandfather was no wizard, but he was a businessman and a poet. He spoke nine languages, including Esperanto. He was born during the time of the smallpox epidemic. We still have many of his poems, and a large number of songs that he wrote and tried to get published in New York and Chicago. He lived in a huge old house that he bought from the T. Eaton Company and built near Libau on the edge of the marshes. When they tore down the house many years after his death, my Uncle Bill, who lived in the house until its demolition, found a manuscript in the old roll-top desk grandfather had used. He gave it to me because he knew I was a writer and would take care of it. I have kept it all these years, but now that the family's story must be told I offer it to you.

BALDUR'S SONG

The first day of all the days I remember was a day in which a cow mooed in the other end of the house. I didn't know it was a cow at the time, but I remember I was affected by the sound. I had actually never had a thought before that moment, and I was surprised by the clarity and power of my thinking. I don't know whether I actually thought something had mooed, but I can still conjure the exact moment of the moo, and the sense of amazement I had at that moment. The memory of my mother's breast is only a moment behind that memory, and the feeling that I was complete and whole, a creature that produced and absorbed milk and was warm and comfortable except for the moo that intimated that there was something in the distance, something that was not me quite exactly, and that did not provide me milk and was not warm.

Everything was blurred at that time, the big clumsy face of my father, the roof of the cabin in which we lived, the fuzzed and chaotic face of others who appeared for moments when I was awake, but who entered my dreams much more clearly. I dreamed at that time, and I could not tell the difference between my dreams and the actual world, and I have to confess that I still can't tell with any accuracy. My next memory is pouring water into my brother's mouth. We are only fourteen months apart, and I suppose I must have become much more sophisticated than when I heard that moo, but everything in between has vanished as an actual memory and has been replaced by my mother's versions. She made me a baby book that I still have along with a lock of my golden hair, and I have to tell you that through everything that has passed since then, I am still vain about the beauty of my infant hair.

But I was her first-born and she loved me inordinately, as mothers love their first-born, and everything I did was a narrative, everything a story that was her story of her first-born, but which confuses things for me because I don't know whether I actually remember or whether I am rehearsing my mother's narratives. Luckily, I had a brother soon after and she bought another baby book for him and began his narrative. My narrative was over, and there were another five beyond us to begin their own narratives.

But this is my story. One day, the second actually conscious moment of my life, I looked at my baby brother in his crib, and decided he must be thirsty. I went to the water bucket that stood on a shelf near the stove. I filled the dipper and asked him whether he was thirsty. As I remember, he answered yes he was, so I poured the entire full dipper into his open mouth. My mother, who was never far away, rescued my brother and I was for the first time aware that I might not be fully admired and loved. I learned at that moment the possibility of guilt, but I must confess that I never felt guilt. My brother had declared his need for water and I had satisfied it. I still find it impossible to repent.

But that opened the possibility to dream and I found out that I was hopelessly removed from the Eden of my first memories. My baby book reveals that my mother was still in love with her first-born, but she was now spreading her undeniable goodness out to a world I felt had no right to it.

I remember next that the house was filled with people. The cows lived at one end of the house and the people lived at the other end. Everybody except my mother, my grandmother, my brother and me were sick. Every few days, somebody disappeared and never came back. All the women cried desperately, and they hugged my brother and me and squeezed us so that we tried to avoid them as much as we could. I remember being taken out for a walk by somebody who might have been an uncle, but who died before I could be sure of his name. He showed me the bodies piled on the roof of the house. He said we would bury them in the spring when the ground was soft enough to dig graves. He named them, and I knew the names. I thought of them as intermediaries between the world of the living and the world of the dead. I thought when spring came, they would come down from the roofs and tell us what they had learned, but that never happened. Later, he too slept on the roof, and had no more stories to tell.

Then one day, the winter was over. The frozen ice on the lake melted. The birds came back in an unbelievable profusion, blackbirds and seagulls and ducks. The lake was filled with fish and everything promised joy. But just a minute. Everything slowed down. Suddenly there was room in my heart for hundreds of memories. I couldn't sleep at night because my mind was flooded by the events of the day, and when I did sleep I dreamed and the dreams were as bright as the memories of the day. My father wrote letters late into the night, strange squiggles on paper that I loved to look at. He told me that he could send them all the way to Iceland and people there would know what he said. It seemed impossible. There was a mail carrier only once a month, and my mother said it was too expensive to send letters to people who didn't know who you were or who had forgotten you. She said you could buy a gallon of milk for the cost of a stamp, and I sided with her. I wanted milk, not squiggles that were going to be carried across the sea to people who didn't care.

But back to my story. The sun came out. The lake melted and as it melted it sang a strange crystalline song like the sound of glass breaking, though at the time I had never heard glass breaking and I still feel that glass breaking is like the sound of a melting lake. The sun came out, and though there had been plenty of sun during the months of winter it was a different kind of sun. That early sun was a cold and distant light that had no warmth in it, but this new sun was hot, like a mother holding her first-born.

The people who had been resting on the roof were taken down and holes were dug in the earth and they were placed in the holes. For weeks I had been expecting to speak to them, but instead they were put in boxes and deposited in holes in the earth. Even my uncle was sullen and refused to speak, even though I addressed him by name. I think now that I might have offended him. I couldn't remember whether his name was Gusti or Gisli and I may have offended him by calling him by the wrong name. Later I found out that his name was Grimsi, but by then it was way too late.

I was glad that they didn't take them away. They planted everyone in a field that was mostly sand, and they didn't plant them very deep. I used to go to the graves and talk to the dead people who whispered so softly that you had to put your ear on the sand above them to hear what they had to say. Most of them were sad that they had spent so much time on the roofs and no one had given them time to explain where they had gone before they buried them. My uncle asked me to dig him up and move his bones. He wanted to be buried back in Iceland, but I was only a little boy and I couldn't send his bones across the ocean. I asked my father to do it instead, but he only said there was plenty of time for my uncle's bones. The dead are in no rush, he said, and he made me promise that I would ask my grandson when I had one, to take care of that request.

The children whispered to me through the small layer of sand. They were frightened that coyotes might come and eat their bones, and then they would have no voices and no bodies to take with them when the final trumpet was sounded. I promised to help them, and I watched many hours each day to see that their graves were safe. After a while they stopped talking to me, and even though I called them by name, they refused to answer.

But the sun that morning was a wonder. The lake was covered with small waves and the sun glinted off the top of every wave. My father spread his nets out in the lake as far as he could walk and the fish were so eager to be caught they jumped over the sidelines in order to be part of the catch. My mother and the other women made a great fire and they cleaned the fish and boiled them, and we all ate until we were so full that we could eat no more. Somebody thought we should thank the Lord for this gift, but we had no minister, and the only man who could recite the prayer of thankfulness had walked to Winnipeg to buy flour and had not returned.

Nobody returned. The disease that had put people on the tops of houses was named. Smallpox. Nobody could enter the community and no one could leave. I hate to confess that it didn't bother me. My mother and my father were alive. I had lost a cousin who had died so quickly that I had never actually met him, but I had learned to whistle. There were many fine singers in the community but no whistlers. I was taught by an English doctor who had sorted out who had to go and lie on the rooftop and who could stay in his bed. He taught me to whistle the "Ode to Joy," and he told me this would be a gift to my people. And so I became a kind of totem figure, the miraculous child who could perform music. I had a strange sort of memory and I could whistle any music that I had ever heard even once. I could also sing, and was often called on to do so when the community gathered, though I was nervous about singing in public.

I thought in those days that we were rich, because our house was always full of people. We had working girls who helped take care of us and who helped my mother clean the house and we had hired men who took care of horses and threw me and my brother high in the air and caught us so that we squealed and demanded they do it again. I didn't know these were people who had no place to go and were grateful for food to eat and a roof over their heads.

But the world was full of food in those days. Moose came down to the streams and practically begged you to shoot them and provide food for everybody. Prairie chickens came in the fall and nested in the trees so that they broke the branches, and we were sent out with sticks to knock them out of trees and bring their bodies to the women who plucked and cleaned them and put their bodies into barrels and salted them.

I have too many memories of those days. I remember that my mother taught me and my brother to play leapfrog on the lawn in front of our house. I remember that she got some seeds for hollyhocks and they flowered red and yellow and white on the south side of the house. I remember that suddenly we had a sister, though nobody had prepared us for that event and we didn't know what to do with such a strange occurrence. Her name was Asta. She had to be picked up when she cried, and she had to be sung to almost all the time. I was called on to whistle every day, and she took everything for granted. My brother and I were amazed at the simple fact of being alive at all, and it had never crossed our minds that we had any claim on the world in general, but this sister made demands. She had to be given what she wanted. If she wanted me to whistle, I would have to whistle. My brother who simply loved everybody was called on to provide love. And she wouldn't pee in the pot if anyone else were in the room.

We had never thought of the possibility of privacy before. Our house had rooms, but there were only the hints of where the walls might be at some time in the future. Even the bathroom, which was simply the place where the pee pot was kept in the day and where the slop bucket gathered potato peels and apple cores until it was emptied in the evening, had only a hanging sheet to ensure modesty. And we had never thought of modesty before. It was a strange and terrifying notion. Our bodies, which had never been anything but the external manifestation of our thoughts, suddenly took on new shapes. They needed to be sheltered. They were suddenly vulnerable. They could be damaged by the eyes of people who looked at them. And other bodies suddenly seemed exotic. Could strange and secret thoughts be revealed by seeing those bodies?

The new teacher was staying with us. She lived behind a door that was protected by a sheet. We set out to try to see her by crawling under the sheet when she was dressing. We saw only an ordinary body, fully dressed, but the teacher was so upset that we had seen her that she moved away, and she was replaced by a cousin who didn't care what we saw. But we decided then that there was some mystery involving women that we were too young to know and that would probably become clear later.

My father built us a new house that had no room for cows in it. They had to go out and live in a shed, and they didn't like that at all. They mooed as loud as they could, but my father was unmovable. The cows had to stay out in their new shed. The horses didn't even have a shed. They had only a lean-to that was attached to the cowshed, but they didn't complain.

A lmost every day I was sent to town to get something from the store, and I remember one occasion that changed my life. I was going to get some number nine yarn for my mother. I always walked past the graves where the people who had been on the roof were buried. On this particular day I had decided to whistle for the under-ground people so that they would not be so lonely. I was whistling the "Ode to Joy" when a girl's voice said to me, "They can't hear you, you know. They're dead."

The girl was standing behind a tree so that I could not see her face, but it was a small tree, and I could see parts of her on either side. What was amazing was that she spoke in English. At school we had to speak that strange flat language, but nobody spoke it anywhere else.

"I know they're dead," I told her, speaking in Icelandic, "but that doesn't mean that they don't like music."

"I don't know what you said," she answered in English. "I don't speak Icelandic."

I didn't know before that moment that anybody in the world didn't speak Icelandic. I tried my English and was amazed I could speak it outside the schoolhouse.

"Even if they're dead they still like music," I said.

"I live in Winnipeg," she told me, still hiding her face behind the tree. "In Winnipeg, the dead stay put and they neither speak nor listen."

I had heard of Winnipeg, and I knew that people sometimes went there, but it was far away. Only people with very important reasons went to Winnipeg. I knew people who had been to Winnipeg, but I had never met anyone who came from there except for the school-teacher. I walked up to the tree and tried to peek around it, but she kept her face averted until I stepped back and she could hide behind the tree again.

I sat down on the grass and waited. I knew she couldn't stay behind the tree forever, and if I just waited she would have to show me her face. It was late in the afternoon and the sun was low in the sky. I remembered that I had to buy number nine yarn for my mother, and I would have to go soon or the store would be closed. After a few minutes she popped out from behind the tree and looked at me. She was the prettiest girl that I had ever seen. Her hair was brown and her eyes were bright green. I knew in that moment that I would never have any peace in my life. I would have to think about her every minute until I joined the people from the roof.

"How long will you stay?" I asked her, thinking I would have to go to Winnipeg if she returned there.

"I don't know," she said. "My father has been sent here by the Government of Manitoba. He is the Inspector."

"What does he inspect?" I asked.

"I don't know," she said. "I have never asked him."

"Will you go to school?"

"Yes."

"I have to go," I told her. "I have to buy some number nine yarn for my mother from the store."

"I have a secret," she said.

"What is the secret?"

"If I told you it wouldn't be a secret anymore."

"What's your name?"

"Lara," she said, and she ran off as fast as she could, across all the graves and into the path through the bush beyond. I wanted to catch her and warn her against wolves and bears and tell her she needed me to protect her, but it was clear she could run faster than me, so I went to the store and bought the number nine yarn and took it home to my mother.

"The Inspector has arrived," I told her.

"Yes," she said. "I know. Where is the yarn?"

I handed her the yarn and said, "The Inspector has a daughter."

"Yes," my mother answered, "and the less said about that the better."

My mother was the best of all mothers, but I knew somehow that I would profit little by telling her of my encounter with Lara. Lara! I wanted to shout out the name. Lara! Lara! The name rang like a bell in my head.

My father, who had just come in from the yard where he had been seaming-on his nets, entered the fray in an unusual way. "You be nice to her," he told me. "She doesn't have a mother." My father never contradicted my mother. His way of getting through the world was to avoid every kind of confrontation, even when he was undeniably in the right. "I'm sorry," he said a dozen times a day, even when others such as my mother should have been the sorry ones.

"Leave well enough alone is what I say," my mother retorted. "There is plenty of misery in this world without seeking it out."

My father said that he was sorry, but he didn't elaborate, so it was impossible to know whether he was sorry for having contradicted my mother or was just generally sorry at all the misery in the world.

This was the best spring that had ever happened in the world. The smallpox had ended. The ice was gone from the lake. Birds of every kind were back. Sometimes there were so many ducks flying north that the sky was darkened and the only sound was the whirring of wings. Crocuses bloomed even before all the snow was gone, and wake-robins blossomed in the roots of the willow trees. School was out, and while I might normally have been happy about that, it meant there was no certain place that I could meet Lara. I had mentioned my encounter with Lara near to the cemetery in what I thought was an offhand manner, but my brother was not deceived.

"You are in love!" he shouted, and would have told the whole world if I hadn't bribed him with the pocketknife I had received for my birthday, and I knew he craved. It struck me then that he must himself be in love or he would not have known the symptoms.

But all of this was forgotten a week later when I went to speak to the people from the roof in the graveyard. They had given up asking me questions or replying to the questions I asked them, but I still felt I could say things there that I could not say anywhere else. I had just been confessing my love of Lara to the spirit of my uncle, Gusti, or whatever his name was, when somebody blew into my ear. Now it is an unusual thing when somebody blows into your ear when you are not expecting it, and I suppose I reacted too strongly, leaping to my feet and jumping away.

Lara was standing there, or rather, leaning over, as she had to blow into my ear. "Do you really love me?" she asked.

"Yes," I said. "That is the unfortunate position I find myself in."

"We shall have a wonderful tragic love affair," she said. "I can see it all now. You will become a sailor and travel the ends of the earth, and I will have a series of exotic lovers, but whenever we meet, we will maintain our own sweet innocent love. We will listen to whip-poorwills and swim in cold lakes and tell each other stories about small animals. And at the end of our lives, we will travel to the northern end of the lake, to the purest wilderness, and we will be purified."

"Maybe we will marry and have twenty-three children," I suggested.

"No, I don't think so. But you may kiss me."

And so I kissed her, the single most important and beautiful kiss in my life. No kiss could have been more innocent and more erotic in the history of the world. I knew in that kiss all the pain I was destined to receive, but also all the joy that was to be my lot. And then I kissed her again and she pulled back and ran away into the forest at the other end of the graveyard.

I didn't see her again that year, because her father had to go back to the city to inspect things there. She wrote me one brief letter after she left, but she didn't mention love and she didn't evoke the memory of that kiss. She commented on the weather, and spoke of the blue coats that were all the style in the city. She said she was allergic to cats, but that she had nevertheless taken home a kitten she had found. And she signed her letter "with fondest regards."

It wasn't much to build on, but I took heart. She had written, and that was something. I wrote back to her and told her that the dead people were sulking and refusing to talk. I wrote about the trees around the graveyard and described several of the people who had recently come to live in Gimli.

For a while, people were leaving Gimli to go to other places, some to North Dakota, some to Saskatchewan, some even going back to Iceland, but then there was a sudden surge of new people, more than enough to make up for those who had left. Sometimes they just moved into the houses of those who had left, and sometimes they lived with other people until they could clear their own land and build themselves a house.

I knew I was not going to stay. I was not going to be either a farmer or a fisherman. I would have to learn to speak proper English so I could move to the city and become someone of importance so that I could woo Lara. So I hung around the stores and when I heard people speak English, I spoke to them to get practice. I found all the English books at the school and I read them all. They introduced me to a strange world of knights and ladies, to African cannibals, to worlds of commerce and to gold rushes. I had never heard of any of these things before, and they were a wonder. I thought I would have to go abroad and see these things for myself.

But I was busy at home. My mother had produced two more brothers for me, and there was not much room left in our small house. There was not much room in the school either. Many new children had arrived from Iceland, and they knew no English at all. The teacher had to train them from scratch, and it fell to me to do more teaching than learning. The teacher assigned me a boy named Ulfar who was the biggest boy in the school. He was bigger than most of the men in town, and he was slow moving and slow thinking, with yellow hair and bright blue eyes. She also assigned me a girl named Elin who was bouncy and pretty and bright. Each morning the three of us left the school and went to the house of the widow Thorgilsdottir where I taught them English for two hours. Then the widow gave us lunch and we went back to the school to learn mathematics and history and geography.

My mother complained of the smallness of our house, and so my father and some of his friends brought some lumber and added a room for the smaller brothers to sleep in. The logs of the wall were chinked with mud, but still the wind whistled through and the boys complained bitterly of the cold. Our sister had her own room right beside the stove, so she was always warm. The boys wanted to sleep in the room with the sister, but she would not allow that. Finally, all four of us brothers shared the same bed for the winter, and my father promised he would make the room warmer for the next year.

One day my father announced we would be going to Winnipeg, just he and me. My brother thought he should go as well but someone had to take care of the cows and that someone turned out to be him. We left on a sunny day in mid-September. The year was 1890 and the teacher had explained that New Iceland was now part of the province of Manitoba. Many people were not happy about being part of Manitoba, but my father was not one of them. He welcomed the new Municipality of Gimli, and he had told my mother he intended to run for the council. I gathered that our trip to Winnipeg had something to do with politics, but my father would not tell me. He just said, "Be patient. It will all become clear soon enough."

My mother had packed lunches for us and we left early because we were to walk all the way to Selkirk the first day. We followed the colony road that wound around creeks and through forests that had not been cleared. There were many farms along the route, and the farmers had built their houses near the road. My father kept stopping to chat with farmers who happened to be on the road, either in ox carts or on horseback. I was worried we wouldn't get all the way to Selkirk and would have to sleep in the open with the wolves.

We took our first break at Boundary Creek. My father explained that this creek had marked the boundary of Manitoba and New Iceland, but that it was now just a creek like any other. We crossed at a small footbridge along a path that deviated from the main road. We had a cup of coffee and ate the first of our sandwiches. The trees were full of birds, prairie chickens migrating south to the United States. Back home they had filled the trees each night until they broke the branches and they were so tame that we could knock them out of the trees with sticks. Now, they were not so many, but they still made a loud noise as they took off from the trees. Every so often we would startle a mule deer, and we saw plenty of foxes and coyotes. My father told me that if we met a black bear I was to be perfectly quiet and back up along the trail until we were out of sight. We walked for a long time until we came to Netley Creek. Recent rains had washed out the bridge, but a man with a boat offered to ferry us across. He and my father argued about the cost, and in the end my father gave him some money and a plug of chewing tobacco.

The creek was broad, as wide as any river, and flights of mallards and teals followed the curve of the creek. Muskrats and beaver swam in the waters, and the man with the boat informed us that the creek was the best place to find crayfish and minnows to use as bait. We had no time to fish, though, and as soon as we were across we set out again. A few miles further on, we came to a settlement called Clandeboye. It was a collection of about a dozen buildings, a small store, a blacksmith's shop, a stable and a church hall. My father stopped at the store and we were directed to a house that would provide us with supper for a small fee.

We sat at a table with three other travellers. They had come all the way from Hecla, and this was their third day of travelling. We agreed to go together to Selkirk after supper. The food was wonderful. We had big slabs of venison with potatoes and gravy, a couple of chickens and saskatoon pie for dessert. The woman who ran this house was a large, heavy woman who laughed almost continuously. I was very tired, and I fell asleep in my chair. But then she came with coffee, and I had a steaming mug with lots of cream and several spoons of sugar. The coffee woke me up and I was anxious to get going, because it was already getting dark.

Our new companions were two very tall brothers named Siggi and Villi and a cousin named Thor who was no taller than me. They spoke in a rapid singsong that was hard to understand. There was only a sliver of moon, and so the road was dark. We could see the lights of farmhouses and that helped. The smallest of the men walked with me, and explained that they had only recently arrived from Iceland and were going to Winnipeg to find work on the railway. None of them spoke any English, but they were delighted to learn of my proficiency and kept asking me to teach them phrases. They were not good students and forgot each phrase almost as soon as they committed it to memory.

I whistled the "Ode to Joy" for them, and they were happy and kept asking me to whistle Icelandic songs for them. They joined in with the words and the time passed so quickly that we were in Selkirk before I realized it. Selkirk was a large town with broad streets. There were people everywhere, hurrying along and speaking in several languages that I did not recognize. I saw several groups of Indians in bright costumes, many of them wearing fur though it was not cold.

My father shook hands with our companions and agreed to meet them the following day to continue the trip to Winnipeg. He told them he would go with them to the railway to talk to the people there. He reassured them that many Icelanders were working for the railway, so they would have no trouble making themselves understood. Then they went on to the hotel and we went down a side street to a house right beside the river.

My father knocked at the door, and a man in his underwear motioned us in.

"This is your uncle Halli," my father said, "and this is Baldur Arnason," and he patted me on the head to indicate that I was the bearer of that august name. I knew my own name, of course, but I don't think I had ever heard it mentioned so formally. Certainly, my father had never called me anything but Baldur.

"Come in Arni, and you too, Baldur Arnason," the man named Halli said. "Gudrun will be here in a minute. She is next door where she has been delivering a child, a healthy boy, but he is doing fine, so she will soon be here."

As soon as he had finished speaking, she arrived as if suddenly conjured from nowhere. Gudrun looked remarkably like my mother, so much so that if I hadn't known that I was in Selkirk and my mother was at home I would have mistaken her.

"Gudrun," my father said, "here is your nephew Baldur Arnason."

"He is big for his age," she replied. "And he looks like you. How is my sister?"

"Pretty good," my father told her. "She will come to see you as soon as she stops having babies." Then he turned to me and said, "This is your mother's twin sister. Give her a kiss."

I did kiss her, or rather she kissed me, a perfunctory peck on the cheek. This was the first that I knew that my mother had a sister. I was put to bed almost immediately but I managed to ask my father about it before I was left alone.

"She has five sisters," he told me, and left.

Alone in a strange dark room I pondered this amazing news. If there were that many sisters, then there might be brothers as well. And if they were all married there must be many children, cousins who I had never suspected existed. I tried to imagine these strange relatives, but try as I might I could not conjure any image of them, and I must have fallen asleep because I was awakened by the smell of coffee and the barking of a small dog that had crawled onto the bed beside me.

"Shut up, Lappi," my father told the dog. "And you had better get dressed and come down for coffee. We have a good day's travel to get to Winnipeg."

"Do they have children?" I asked him. "Halli and Gudrun, do they have children?"

"No," my father replied. "And it would be best not to mention it to Gudrun. It's a sore point with her, and she doesn't like to talk about it."

Breakfast was wonderful: eggs and heart-shaped waffles and bacon and hot coffee. Gudrun asked me questions about my brothers and sisters, and I answered as best I could. I realized then that I didn't pay much attention to the younger ones. I couldn't remember what grades they were in at school, and I certainly had no ideas what their dreams and plans might be. Lappi seemed to have taken a liking to me. He sat right beside me at the breakfast table, and followed me wherever I went.

They locked Lappi in the house when we were leaving, because Halli said that Lappi had a habit of following people and then not being able to find his way home. We met the men from Hecla at the hotel and set out for Winnipeg. There was much more traffic now than we had faced the day before. Horses pulled wagons with loads of vegetables and cans of milk. Oxen trudged along pulling carts loaded with hay and straw. A man dressed in some sort of uniform drove a democrat pulled by horses. Two elegantly dressed young women rode in it.

After a short while, we came to Lower Fort Garry. My father explained that there were two Fort Garrys, and this was the larger of the two. It existed to trade furs with the Indians, and there were certainly a lot of Indians camped around it. Their teepees looked just as the teacher had described them, but I had never seen one before. Smoke rose from a dozen fires, and the men all carried rifles in their hands.

The nearer we got to the city, the heavier the traffic grew. The Red River carts squeaked and moaned as if they were in pain. And voices cajoled horses and oxen to greater efforts. Everybody seemed in a great hurry. The first buildings we saw were small shed-like structures, no more impressive than the outbuildings on the farms or the houses in Selkirk, but as we entered the city itself, we saw huge buildings, several stories high. They had elaborate decorations, gargoyles leering from the corners and carved grapevines on pillars. Main Street was extremely wide, and everywhere buildings were under construction. Men were digging trenches along the sides of the street; sewers, my father told me. The noise was incredible. I had never imagined so much shouting, so much squawking of machinery and bleating of animals. Dogs ran loose in the streets everywhere.

On our way to the railway office, we passed through the market area. Everywhere there were stands with merchandise for sale. I had never in my life seen so much food displayed. People were buying live pigs in a pen. Chickens and ducks were displayed, both alive and dead, rabbits and prairie chickens and deer. There was every kind of vegetable, and many that I had never seen before, large multicoloured gourds, tiny cabbages that seemed immature, great dark green kinds of lettuce, and small orange things I could give no name to.

It was only a small way from the market to the CPR railway station. Just as we entered, a train arrived, blasting its whistle and pouring out spouts of steam. I had never seen a train before except in pictures, and I had no idea the engine could be as big or as frightening. The train stopped and people climbed out of it onto the platform. All the people on the train were dressed in fine clothing. Many carried either canes or umbrellas, and the women all had bags and leather cases. We hurried past these people and down some stairs and into an office. My father explained that these Hecla men were looking for work, but his explanation was unnecessary. The uniformed man in the office shouted out the name Helgi, and in a few minutes Helgi appeared, speaking Icelandic. He hired them on the spot, and we shook hands with them until Helgi took them away.

"Now," my father said. "Now our adventure begins."

And that was indeed the beginning of my first adventure. My father took me to the home of a woman who he called Mrs. Thorsteinson. She lived on a street that was named Ruby Street. She was nearly blind and almost completely deaf. My father told her I was a good boy, and that I could be trusted to go out and buy groceries and bring her all the change. I would empty the chamber pots every morning and stoke the furnace and carry in wood. He spoke to her in a loud voice.

"Baldur," he said, to me. "Come over and meet Mrs. Thorsteinson. You will be staying with her for a while, and I want you to do whatever she asks you to do."

I said hello, but apparently not loud enough for her to hear. She looked expectant, waiting for me to say something. I drew in a deep breath and spoke in as loud a voice as I could muster: "Hello."

"Yes," she said. "Hello, indeed."

My father told me he would be gone for some time, and in the meanwhile I was to behave myself and not do anything that would make him ashamed of me. I promised, and he left. Mrs. Thorsteinson ordered me to call her "Hilda," and she led me to my room, a small room with slanting walls on the second story. It was dark and cold, but it had a window so I could look down on the street below. What I could see from the window was a lively scene. Young women dressed in elegant costumes strolled down the streets, holding parasols. Men met them and engaged them in conversation. Sometimes the young woman would take the arm of the man who had approached her and they would go off arm in arm around the corner. Sometimes a sort of argument would ensue, and then several young women would congregate and argue with the man until he went away. It was, all in all, a perplexing scene.

Soon after, Hilda called me down for coffee and *kleinurs*, doughnuts in the shape of figure eights, along with toast and raspberry jam. However blind she was, it didn't seem to slow her down. After coffee, I asked if I might go out to look around the neighbourhood. She told me that I might go, but warned me not to enter any of the houses, even if I was invited. I was unaccustomed to refusing offers of hospitality, but I agreed.

The scene on the street was even livelier than I had been able to discern from the window. Music blared from the windows of many of the houses, mostly piano music played on instruments that were out of tune, but sometimes concertinas and violins or guitars. Most of the men appeared to be drunk, though it was only mid-afternoon. Many of them carried bottles with them and drank from the bottles in the middle of the street. There was more swearing than I had ever heard before, and much of it was provided by lovely young women who looked like schoolteachers.

A few blocks further on, the atmosphere was much more quiet. There were several churches, and couples strolled quietly while children played on the lawns they passed. Carriages hurried along the street with matched teams and harness that had been decorated with shining gold and silver bells. The people in the carriages were all well-dressed. I heard the sounds of hooves beating, and only noticed a carriage that would have run over me had I not leaped to safety. A young woman's face looked out me, and I could scarcely believe my eyes.

"Lara," I shouted but it was far too late. An arm waved from the carriage and a white handkerchief floated to the ground. I ran to pick it up before anyone else could, but when I looked around there was no one else near. The handkerchief had a small rose embroidered in one corner, and it smelled of some wonderful perfume. I tucked it inside my shirt and headed home. It was becoming dark, but the action on the street seemed even livelier than before.

When I got back to my room, I found an elderly man asleep in the second bed in the room. He was a large man with a huge white beard and a shock of white hair. He wore a checked shirt and pants of some material I had not seen before. His braces were bright red. And he wore an equally bright red necktie. A guitar leaned against the headboard of the bed. He was snoring when I arrived and continued to snore for several minutes. Finally, he opened his eyes and looked at me.

"And who are you?" he asked.

"I am Baldur," I replied. "Baldur Arnason. And I think this is my room."

"Well, yes it is," he said. "In a manner of speaking. Yet it is also my room. You see, this house is a rooming house. And this is a room. The delightful Hilda rents space. There is not much spare room in Winnipeg, and so we must all share what there is." He took a handkerchief from his pocket and blew his nose loudly into it. The guitar shone in the late rays of the setting sun through the window.

"Snuff," he said. "It's terrible stuff. Eats away the lining of your nose. Take my advice and stay away from it. Or if you will not stay away from it, pass me that package on the table and I will share it with you." The snuff was in a round green box with the name Copenhagen on it. I passed it to him, and he took a pinch between his thumb and his forefinger and inhaled it deeply. He rolled his eyes and sighed, then passed the box to me. I knew of snuff because several of the fishermen in New Iceland sniffed it, but I had never been offered it before. My father had spoken of new adventures and I thought I might just as well begin here. I took the snuff, squeezed it between my fingers and inhaled.

Immediately, I sneezed the greatest sneeze I have ever accomplished then or since. My eyes began to water and I sneezed again and again. I thought that my head might explode. I decided at that moment that I would refrain from snuff as long as I was in this world. The old man laughed and offered me another pinch. I refrained and he said, "Well, now you know what snuff is. My name is Hannes." And he extended his hand.

I shook it. New Iceland had many hand-shakers. Men shook hands when they met and when they parted. So did women. Men and women shook hands with children, but children did not shake hands with each other. They also blessed each other on meeting and parting. The English people I had seen in Winnipeg did not shake many hands, and they certainly did not bless each other.

I thought since Hannes and I were apparently friends now, I should try to gain from him some knowledge of this place called Winnipeg.

"Why are there so many pretty young women walking in the streets and meeting men and taking them by the hand and leading them into houses?"

"Ah!" he said. "That is not so easy to explain. These women are streetwalkers, though they are often called by other less pleasant names. It is their employment to give men pleasure. You see—" and here he leaned forward and spoke to me in a confidential way—"you see, Winnipeg has grown enormously in the last few years. In order to grow it has had to attract many men to work here, building houses and stores, making roads, digging sewers, driving carts, selling merchandise, and doing all the things that are required to build a city. And many of these men have left their wives and girlfriends behind, or else arrived without either wife or girlfriend. And they are lonely, and sometimes they drink too much and they want love and companionship. These girls provide it for them for a fee."

"They are generous," I said, "going out of their way to help the lonely men."

"Well, it's not quite simple generosity. These are not church workers. In fact, what they offer is condemned by the church as sinful."

"I hear music coming from those houses. I would like to go inside and hear it better."

"What does Hilda tell you about those houses?"

"She says I am not to enter them."

"Well, that settles it then. You should stay out of them, at least until you are somewhat older and understand more about the nature of the world." And he put a captain's hat on his head and said that we should get down for supper before the other lodgers arrived and ate everything.

"Would you teach me to play the guitar?" I asked Hannes.

"Have you music in you?" he asked. I whistled a few bars of the "Ode to Joy," and he said, "Yes, of course. You have the gift that is not given to many. But that gift can also be your undoing, so if I teach you, you will have to take moral instruction from me."

I agreed. At that moment I would have sold my soul to the devil to learn how to play the guitar.

"Come along," he said, and we walked down the stairs together.

That night we began our lessons. Hannes showed me several chords and I practised them. It was difficult at first, twisting my fingers into odd shapes, but after a while I got the hang of it. "Just practise the chords," he told me. "Don't try to play music until you learn more."

I agreed, but the next day he went off and left me with the guitar. I did not leave the house. I practised every moment, and when Hannes returned that evening, I could play a passable version of the "Ode to Joy."

"Didn't I tell you not to play any tunes until I told you to?" he said.

"Yes, but I figured this one out by myself." I was more than a little proud of my accomplishment.

"Here," he said. "We are going to do scales. When you can do all of your scales, then we will get to tunes. In the meanwhile, if you want to fool around with tunes you can use this," and he pulled from his pocket a harmonica wrapped in a red handkerchief. He put it to his mouth and began to play "Turkey in the Straw," then "Sweet Betsy from Pike" and finally "The Derby Ram." I had never heard any of these tunes before and I made him sing me the words. Then he showed me how to breathe and use my tongue to make individual notes. I was prepared to give up the guitar in favour of this magical instrument, but Hannes said no, I had better learn the guitar first, then I would be able to play many instruments.

To tell you the truth, what with playing the instruments and learning the words to songs, I completely forgot about my father who had brought me to this place and who had then disappeared. I scarcely thought of my poor mother and all those brothers and sisters back in New Iceland. I had not forgotten Lara. She floated in the back of my consciousness whatever I was doing, but now I started to feel guilty that I had not gone out and searched for her. I determined I would continue to practise, but that I would devote two hours each day to searching for her.

The next morning at breakfast, I asked Hilda if she knew when my father would return. She said no, she did not know for sure but that it would probably not be very soon. She did not know where he had gone.

Later that evening, Hannes told me that he had gone on the railway to The Lakehead, Fort William, to be precise. The railroad had suddenly decided to hire stevedores to help load grain. He didn't know my father, and he wasn't certain where he was, but he said that was the most likely place. The railway was offering huge salaries, and half the men in the city had already gone.

Then the next day, I received a letter from my father. He asked me to be patient and told me that he had found a way to make a small fortune, and that when he returned, all of our lives would be much better. He warned me not to drink hard liquor and to stay out of the houses where the young women lived.

I resolved right then to find out what hard liquor tasted like, and to see what went on in those forbidden houses. I was generally an obedient boy, but I always wanted to see things for myself. I had tried snuff, and though I was not anxious to try it again, I had gained certain knowledge. Hannes had allowed me to progress to the point where I could play the guitar with confidence, and I had learned the words to several dozen songs. And I had begun my search for Lara. Unfortunately, we had several days of rain, and the streets were swimming in mud. The horses pulling carts were covered in it, and the men on the streets had mud sticking to their boots so that they looked as miserable as the horses. A cold wind from the north made the city entirely miserable.

Then on one of the coldest and most miserable days I ducked into a church to get out of the wind and rain. And there in the church was Lara. She was standing in the first pew with her leg resting on the top of the pew. She appeared to be doing some sort of exercise. She was dressed in a pair of black leggings with a black and white blouse. Her hair was as brown as ever. There was no one else in the church, or at least no one in sight.

I walked down the aisle, and she did not notice me until I was a few feet away. She continued with her exercises.

"Oh," she said. "It's you." Her green eyes were even brighter than I remembered.

"Yes," I answered. "It is indeed me."

"You're far from home."

"Yes. What are you doing?"

"These exercises?"

"Yes."

"I am preparing for a career as a dancer. I shall probably become a ballet dancer and dance in the great capitals of the world. Tell me, do you still love me?"

"Of course. I have been searching the city for you for over a month."

"Well, now that you have found me, what do you propose to do about it?"

"What could I do about anything? I want to talk with you."

"What shall we talk about?" I realized then that I had nothing to say to her, or at least nothing that I could bring to mind at the moment. All my planning had gone into finding her, but I had no idea what I should do once I had found her. I stood there in the church, silent.

"Do you still talk to the dead?" she asked.

"No. They no longer wish to speak. I suppose they have other things to do."

"There's not a lot to do in a graveyard. I should like to think that they would want you to whistle the 'Ode to Joy.'"

"Perhaps. But I have progressed beyond merely whistling. I now play musical instruments. The guitar and the mouth organ for now, but I propose to learn a great many others." The ceiling of the church was high and painted blue with golden stars. It was nearly as cold in the church as it was outside.

"So do you plan to be a musician? Will you play in the great concert halls of the world's great cities or will you entertain on street corners and ask passersby to throw coins into a cup?" It had never before struck me that I would have to be anything in particular. I had hoped to go on living my life as I did now, and the only future I hoped for was one in which Lara would take part. I had not even quite figured out what part she would play, but I thought we would be inseparable. She had finished doing her exercises and she slipped a large black-and-white woollen sweater over her costume.

"May I kiss you?" I asked.

"Yes," she said. "Each time we meet you may kiss me, but not here. You may walk me home and I will kiss you when we get to my house."

It had stopped raining, but it was cold and damp for all that. I took Lara's hand in mine and we walked down the street. We made many turns under the elm trees that lined the streets, and I was soon completely lost.

"Sing me a song," she said, "and not the 'Ode to Joy.'" I sang her "Sweet Betsy from Pike," and when I was finished, she suddenly kissed me and ran up the sidewalk and into a large house with a curved verandah.

"Wait," I shouted. "When can I see you again?"

I'm not sure what she answered. She may have said, "anytime," or she may have said, "never," or she may have said, "tomorrow." The wind that had begun to howl drowned out her words. I went up to the house to look for its number, but it had no number. The street sign at the corner had been torn down, and the street had no name. I began to count my steps and remember in which direction I had turned, but it was soon clear that I knew no more about where I was going than I did about where I had been.

The next day I found the church again. Again, there was no one there. I tried to remember the route we had taken to the house in which Lara lived, but I was soon lost in a maze of streets. I had forgotten Lara's father's name, and so I could not ask anyone for help and direction. Nevertheless, I stalked the street, hoping to catch a glimpse of her. I saw a young woman who looked like her from a distance but on closer look turned out to be someone entirely different.

When I returned that evening I found Hannes in great distress. He had been vomiting, and he coughed incessantly. I tried to ask what was wrong, but he was delirious and spoke only of the valley in Iceland that he had left and the mother who was waiting for his return. I went to talk to Hilda to see whether there was something we could do. She sent me out to find a doctor and gave me an address.

When I arrived at the house, it turned out to be one of those houses where I was forbidden to go. I knocked on the door, and it was answered by a young woman who was barely dressed. I apologized for getting her out of bed. She laughed a loud musical laugh and asked whether I was looking to buy some love and comfort. I told her that I was there for the doctor. Hilda had called him Doctor Smith, and when I asked for him, she laughed even more loudly.

"He's here all right, though I don't think you'll get much help from him." She led me to another room where several men sat drinking whisky from glasses and listening to a boy no older than myself playing the guitar. The doctor was dressed in a black suit, so that he looked more like an undertaker than a doctor.

"Doctor Smith?" I asked.

"Yes," he answered, slurring his words so that he was nearly incomprehensible. "What can I do for you, young fellow? You look healthy enough."

"It's not me." I said, and I blurted out my own assessment of Hannes's health. I told him I was afraid that he would die. I had heard that when death threatens, the dying person thinks only of his mother and the place in which he was born. The doctor stumbled to his feet, though he nearly fell doing so, and he lurched towards the door.

"Come, young fellow," he said, picking up his little black bag from the chair on which it rested. "Lead on. We must rescue this man from what is probably a spectacular hangover, but that is what we doctors are sworn to do." I took his arm to steady him, and led him to the door. The young woman who had let me in was still in her bedclothes.

"Come back when you can stay a little longer," she told me. "You look like you could use a little fun. My name is Flora. Remember my name. You may need it yet."

It was a nightmare getting the doctor to Hilda's house, because he lurched into trees and fell on the sidewalk and didn't want to get up again. When we arrived at Hilda's place, however, he went through a remarkable change. He straightened up, spoke slowly and clearly, and in every way was thoroughly professional. He climbed the stairs without incident, and sat by Hannes's bed. He put his hand on Hannes's head and asked him several questions. Hannes did not answer the questions. Between fits of coughing, he spoke only of his mother.

"This is serious," the doctor told me. "We will have to sit with him until dawn. If he can make it through the night he may survive." And the doctor took from his bag a bottle filled with a green fluid that he poured into a spoon and forced between Hannes's lips.

That was one of the most horrible nights of my life. Hannes roared and wept and coughed. The doctor restrained him as if he were fighting with his soul to keep it from leaving the earth. Finally, near dawn, he fell into a deep sleep. The doctor was hunched over in his chair, also asleep. I must have joined them, because when I woke up sunshine poured through the window, Hannes and the doctor were gone and I was alone. I went down to the kitchen where Hilda was preparing soup for lunch. I asked where Hannes had gone.

"He's gone to a better place than this one," she said. "He could not be saved. The doctor did all that was possible. And don't blame him. He was a fine doctor until the whisky got him, the finest doctor in all of Winnipeg."

"What will happen to Hannes's things?" I asked, thinking of the guitar, and already guilty for thinking about my own selfish needs when Hannes was on his way to join the people under the ground.

"He has nothing," Hilda said. "He sent all his money home to his mother in Iceland. He will have enough to cover the cost of his funeral. You may as well have the guitar because he cannot play it anymore, and he has no family here." Then, as if she had suddenly made a discovery, she said, "Of course, you will have to write a letter to his mother describing his last hours."

I agreed and went upstairs to look at the guitar. It seemed to have new dignity. It sat there gleaming by the bed as if to say, "Now you will have to care for me. Now you have some responsibility in the world." The mouth organ was in the top drawer of the dresser. I opened the drawer and looked at it. I supposed that it was now also mine.

At supper, Hilda confirmed that. She said everything Hannes owned was in his suitcase, and that I could take whatever I wanted and then she would send the rest to the church to be given to the poor. I went back to the room, but at first I couldn't bear to open the suitcase. It seemed like prying. All that was left of Hannes was in that suitcase, and once that was gone there would be no more sign of Hannes in the world except for a wooden cross with his name.

After a while, I reasoned that Hannes would want me to look over his belongings. There might be something I should send to his mother. So I opened the suitcase, which was more of a small trunk with brass fittings on the corners and a brass latch that didn't work. I first removed the clothes. They were all far too large for me, but there was a black suit that looked as if it had never been worn and which I guessed was intended for his burial. I set it aside on his bed to give to Hilda. There were a couple of pairs of socks, some underwear and two shirts. I thought that was all, but then I noticed a sort of tab near the bottom of the trunk. I pulled it, and the bottom of the case lifted so that I could see that it had been a false bottom. Carefully packed into this space were a number of items. The first was an intricately carved box which when I opened it revealed a tiny but elegant chess set. A leather case contained a gold pocket watch with a gold chain and fob. On the fob were carved two hunting dogs. I wound up the watch and it began to tick, and the arms of the watch began to sweep in circles. Another packet contained money, a wad of four-dollar bills, twenty dollars in all.

The biggest surprise, however, was a waterproof wallet containing papers. There were several letters from his mother, and three from a woman named Jona declaring her love for him and wondering when he would be coming home. Some were official-looking letters from the government, but I couldn't figure out what they were. And finally there was a deed for section three, township nineteen, range four east. Apparently Hannes owned a farm, but the numbers gave me no idea of where it might be.

My first impulse was to turn over the contents to Hilda, but she had told me that I could keep whatever was left in the case, so I could presume it to be mine. I knew however that I had little moral right to any of these things, and if the church was correct in its reasoning, I would someday have to account for how these objects had come into my possession. Hilda ran the rooming house, but she didn't seem to be related to Hannes in any family way. In the end, I decided to put all I had found in my own bag, and leave the moral problems to my father when he arrived. He had been gone for nearly two months now, and I was sure he must return soon.

The next day, Hilda told me the money my father had paid for me had run out and that if I didn't find another ten dollars in two days, then I would have to leave. I had no money and the thought of going out into the street terrified me. I had Hannes's money, but I knew I had no moral right to spend it. I could think of no plan, and so I continued walking the streets of the city looking for Lara. I did not find her, but I did find Flora.

"How's my little man?" she asked. We had met on the street in front of the church where I had met Lara. I went there every day hoping that she might return, but she had not.

"It's not so good," I told her, and explained my dilemma. I did not tell her about Hannes and the four-dollar bills, but as I explained my problem, I became increasingly aware of my vulnerability, and my eyes filled with tears.

"Don't worry," she said, "I will take care of you. I have some money and I can pay her bill." She reached into her pocket and brought out ten dollars, which she handed to me.

"Thank you," I said. "I will certainly repay you as soon as my father returns."

"If he returns."

The prospect that my father might not return had never before entered my mind, and I refused to think about it now. "He will return," I assured her. "He has only gone to Fort William to work on the boats."

"Perhaps," she said. "But you would do well to find some way to earn your living until he does return. Can you shine shoes? They are looking for boys at the railway station who can shine shoes."

"I have never shined shoes," I said, "but I think it cannot be too difficult."

"Come by the house tomorrow morning at eight o'clock, and I will have a shoeshining kit for you." Just then a somewhat drunken man came round the corner and called her name. "Eight o'clock," she told me, then she took the fellow by the arm and led him off into the twilight.

Hilda was suspicious of my sudden wealth, but I told her that my father had left that money for me in case of emergency, and I considered being put out in the cold an emergency. She said that I should probably go back to New Iceland, and that she knew of someone who was going there and would be happy to take me. I told her my father's strict orders were that I stay, and I did not want to be disobedient to my father.

I went to my room, played the guitar for a few moments and the mouth organ for another few moments. I counted the money, polished the gold watch and looked at the ivory chessmen. Hannes's chest had vanished and there was no sign that he had ever been there. Yet I still felt as if he were a presence demanding that I do something. Then I remembered the letter to his mother. I found an address on one of the letters that she had sent and sat down to write. I told her of Hannes's illness, of his love for her and his final moments in which he called out to her. I sealed the letter and put it in my pocket. I thought that I should perhaps write to Jona, but I had no idea what I could say. And her expressions of love had been so fervent I was sure she would not have wanted anyone else to read them.

Eight o'clock came early, and I was waiting at the door of the house when Flora came out with the shoeshine kit. She also handed me a note.

"Take this to the manager on the main floor and he will give you a place to work."

I took the note dutifully, and trudged down in the direction of the railway station. The city was relatively quiet, but the station was a hive of activity. People rushed in every direction, and their voices made a babbling like a flock of geese. The manager had an office behind the ticket sellers, and I had to ask one of them to get him for me. She was reluctant to go, but I passed her the note and she took it to him. The manager appeared a moment later. He led me down a long hallway to an area where people milled about waiting for their trains and where arrivals searched for the people who were supposed to meet them.

He led me to a raised bench where people could sit and place their feet on what appeared to be models of upside-down feet. I could see how the system worked.

"This is your station," the manager told me. "Johnny Ashdown has the station across from you and Reuben has the third station." He pointed at a grey-haired black man who was actually polishing somebody's shoes. I was amazed. I had never seen a black man before, though of course I knew they existed. Winnipeg seemed an even more marvellous place where you could find people of different colours. The black man was sweating and he shone in the lights of the station.

Johnny Ashdown was a medium-sized boy wearing a pair of brown breeches, a checked shirt and a cloth cap. He was shouting

"Shoeshine, shoeshine, fifteen cents for a shoeshine." I could see he had noticed me, and that the polite thing to do would be to go over and say hello to him, but I was reluctant. He seemed so capable and assured, and I was about to compete with him for money when I had never shone a shoe in my life before. I opened my kit and took out two tins of polish, one brown and one black, a brush and several pieces of cloth. I watched Ashdown, who now had a customer. He brushed the first shoe, then smeared the shoe with polish with his bare hands. He did the same with the second shoe. Then he brushed the shoes vigorously, and finally he snapped one of his cloths and began to reel it back and forth across the shoe. Finally, he spat on the shoe and gave it a final polish. The customer examined the shoes, seemed pleased and gave Ashdown some money.

Ashdown put the money in his pocket and began to peel an orange. I shouted out, "Shoe polish, shoe polish, fifteen cents for a shoe polish." Soon I too had a customer, a fat man wearing a vest and a hat but no overcoat. He wore a striped shirt and braces. I worked as fast and as hard as I could and was quite proud of the job I had done.

"Thanks, kid," the man said and walked off without paying me. I ran after him to ask for my pay, but he raised his fist and said, "Smarten up, kid, if you want to stay healthy."

Ashdown sauntered over still eating his orange. "Railway dick," he said. "Pinkerton Man. Next time one of them comes by just tell him you're going for a lunch break. Those bastards never pay."

"How do I know who is a railway dick?" I asked him.

"They all look the same. Fat pigs in braces and no overcoat. What's your name?"

"Baldur," I told him. He didn't seem like the kind of person who would want to hear my full name.

"Johnny Ashdown," he said and held out his hand. "In a few years I'm going to own this entire block," and he swung his hand to indicate the city beyond the station.

"Do you think we can make a lot of money shining shoes?" I asked.

"Naw, and don't let the few dollars you get go to your head. Before you go home the manager will drop by and collect half of your earnings."

"Why?" I asked.

"Because he can. And if you don't like it you can go home and not come back."

"What if I don't get any customers?"

"That's just too bad, because he'll collect anyway. And you better have enough for what he thinks is half. Gotta go." And he went back to his station and began to call out his shoeshine song again.

I was indignant, but in no position to protest. After a while I got another customer, and by evening I had shined eight pairs of feet. The manager came by just as Ashdown had predicted. I showed him my earnings, and he took half the money.

"This is not good enough, Baldur," he said. "You'll have to be making double that by the end of the week or I'll have to let someone else have your station. I hired you as a favour to Flora, but you're going to have to earn your keep."

Ashdown was waiting for me by the door as I left. I told him of the manager's threat.

"Naw," he said. "You did good. And you've got one on him. If he does try to fire you just tell him that you're going to bring Flora over to meet his wife and kids. That'll settle him." We walked across the street and stopped in a hotel and ordered coffee. I had never before ordered food in a restaurant and paid for it with my own money.

"The way I figure it," Ashdown said, "is that information is money, but you have to have money to make money. Now I overhear things. I know that a couple of bankers are looking to put up a warehouse on a vacant lot on Princess Street. If I had enough money I could buy the lot and they'd have to pay me double, because they have already sold people space in advance."

"Do you have enough money to buy a lot?"

"Not yet. But soon."

He walked home with me, and when we reached the houses of comfort he asked, "Have you tried them out yet?"

"Of course not. I have been warned away from those houses."

"Yeah," he said. "Well, anyway, I've got to go." And he turned a corner and I watched until he disappeared in the night.

The long hours I worked cut into my search for Lara. I scarcely had any time to wander the streets. On the other hand I now had a friend. I had never had a friend before, except my brother, and he was a brother, not a friend. There is a difference. You can never escape brothers, but you have to be careful with friends. They can leave and that's the end of it. Brothers can get angry or hurt, but no matter what they do, you are still brothers.

Johnny asked me dozens of questions about New Iceland, about my family, about my dreams and fantasies. He made me speak sentences to him in Icelandic and he laughed and said it sounded like a snake hissing. I told him about Lara and he was sympathetic. He had once been in love himself, but one day she had simply moved away without telling him, and so now he didn't take any chances on falling in love.

"Look at you," he said, "walking the streets like some condemned soul. You have no time to be happy. You have your obsession instead of happiness. Now, my obsession is money, and it is an obtainable obsession. But what would you do even if you found her? Even if she pledged her undying love for you, her father would simply whisk her away and that would be the end of it." He put into words my worst fears, and his words haunted me as I searched.

After two weeks, I had earned enough money to pay Flora back. There was still no sign of my father, and I was beginning to worry that he might not indeed ever return. I missed a day at the station because I had caught a cold. The manager was not at all sympathetic.

"You have a job, and that is more important than your cold. Don't miss any more days." I wanted to object, but it seemed pointless. That day I took my letter to Hannes's mother to the post office and mailed it. I imagined that it would travel by train east to Quebec and then it would get on a boat and travel to Iceland. In Iceland, it would be taken by horse to the village in which she lived and she would open it and weep for her dead boy.

That evening after I had finished work and had a cup of coffee with Johnny, I returned home and took the guitar out onto the porch to practise. Somebody had left a book on a bench at the station. The name of the book was *The World's One Hundred Best Songs*. I set out to memorize them all. I preferred "Greensleeves" and "The Streets of Laredo," but I was only a small way into the book and I thought I might find even more wonderful songs in its pages.

I remembered that I had not yet repaid Flora, and the money in my pocket made me uncomfortable. I walked down the street towards the house in which she lived, carrying Hannes's guitar. As soon as I earned enough money, I planned to buy a case for it. Flora was sitting on the porch with several of the other girls. The weather was unseasonably hot. A warm wind from the south made everything seem like the heart of summer. The girls were all dressed in nightclothes, and they stretched and walked around without modesty.

I called to Flora, and she came down the walk to meet me. I passed her the money, and she said, "You didn't have to return it, you know. I gave it to you because I wanted to."

"Well," I said, "I have also returned it because I wanted to."

Several of the girls began to call to me, "Give us a song, young fellow. A song to make us happy."

"Do," Flora said. "Sing us a happy song. His name is Baldur," she added and the girls began to chant, "Baldur, Baldur, Baldur." I was embarrassed, but I tuned the strings of my guitar and I played and sang for them. I sang "You Are My Sunshine" and "I've Been Working on the Railroad" and I ended with "The Red River Valley." When I finished, several of the girls were in tears.

I was just about to go when a large woman in a flowing dress came out onto the porch. The dress was white with pink flowers and small yellow birds. "What's going on?" she asked. "Who was doing that singing?" The girls all vanished like chicks when a hawk flies over.

"Me," I said. "My name is Baldur."

"And mine is Minnie," she said. "This is my house. I own it. Where do you live? What are you doing here?"

I told her that I lived just a few blocks away near Ellice Avenue. I told her that I was staying with Hilda until my father returned and that I was shining shoes at the railway station.

"And how much money do you earn?"

I told her and she mused for a moment. "You are very young."

"Not so very," I answered.

"I will hire you to play music and sing. But you must not take any alcohol and you must leave the girls alone." Then, almost as an afterthought, she added, "Two dollars an evening, take it or leave it."

I knew I should not even enter such a house, but I could earn more money than I could earn shining shoes and I would have my days free to search for Lara.

"I will," I told her. "I can start immediately."

"Well come on then," she said and led me to the same room in which I had found the doctor. He was already there, along with a half-dozen other men. One of the girls was sitting on the knee of a young man dressed formally in a black suit.

"We have a new entertainer," she told the group. "This is Baldur, the Icelandic songbird."

I did a little bow and began to sing "The Darby Ram." The others continued with their drinking as if they hadn't noticed my arrival. I sang several more songs, then announced that I would take a break. The young woman on the knee of the man with the black suit had somehow shifted her robe so that one breast was clearly visible. Now, I have several younger brothers and sisters, so that I knew what a breast looked like, yet there was something quite different about this breast. It did not look like the breast of a mother. It was in some way disturbing, and I was grateful when she moved and covered it from view.

The doctor, who had seemed comatose during my entire performance, now sat up in his chair and congratulated me. He said it was not often that they provided such fine music in this establishment, and did I intend to stay? I told him that the position was only temporary, and as soon as my father returned I would be going back to New Iceland. He brightened at that and said, "Ah, I remember that place. I was there at the time of the smallpox. I went from house to house caring for the dying, though to tell the truth, there wasn't much that I could do. I remember one place where there was cow in the end of the house, and its lowing kept everyone awake." I believed then, as I do now, that the cow was the very cow that had awakened me to consciousness by its mooing.

"It was terrible," he went on. Everywhere there were dying infants and dying older folk. Only the young and the strong survived. Because the ground was frozen and they could not bury the dead, the Icelanders stacked them on the roofs to keep them from the wolves, though even then they had to wrap them tightly so that birds would not do the job."

I asked him to describe the house with the cow and he said, "There's not much to describe. It was a long, narrow log house chinked with clay. The cow lived in one end and the people in the other. But I remember that it was a cold day and I had travelled far. The woman of the house offered me a cup of tea, which I gratefully accepted. When she thought I wasn't looking, she put the cup to her mouth and cleaned it with her tongue. Then she wiped it dry with piece of cloth that was black from use. And I had to drink from that cup and I could have caught the smallpox myself."

"Why did you drink from it?" I asked. "Why didn't you just refuse?"

"Because you cannot refuse a gesture made from the goodness of the heart, even if it risks your own life. That is the law of the frontier, and I live by that law."

I saw in my imagination my mother take the cup and clean it for the doctor. I was proud of her. No matter how bad things were, she always kept up appearances. And now I felt connected to the doctor in the same way that I was connected to Lara. He had been there at the moment of my awakening, and that was a powerful bond.

"Were there any babies in that house?" I asked.

"Yes," he said, "and the most remarkable thing was that one of the babies, a little boy, could whistle."

"What tune did he whistle?"

"I'm not sure there was any tune. But it was remarkable nevertheless."

"How long did you stay in New Iceland?" I asked him.

"About three months," he answered. "And I saw worse sights than that. I went with the police one time to an Indian village across the lake where smallpox was reported. When we arrived at the village, we found dozens of bodies hanging by ropes from the trees. There was still a fire burning in one of the tents, but every person in the place was dead. The final tent held a woman clutching her dead baby to her dead breast. The fire had not yet died, and both of their bodies were still warm. Then the police made a torch and they burned all the tents with the bodies inside them. I cannot sleep at nights, because the sight of all those dead and dying people keeps me awake. I am only happy when the whisky dulls the pain."

The next day I continued my quest for Lara. I had a new plan. I knew there were many Icelanders living in Winnipeg and I decided to find them and see if they could help me. I went first to the railway station to talk to the men who worked on the railway. None of them actually lived in Winnipeg, and so they couldn't help me, but they told me of a hall where Icelanders gathered, and they gave me directions so I could find it. I followed those directions and came to a small white building that doubled as a church and a meeting place. It was much smaller than the church where I had encountered Lara, but there were a number of Icelanders singing there. They called themselves the Winnipeg Icelandic Men's Choir, or at least that is what a notice on the door said. I waited until they finished, and when they were having coffee I walked in and began to talk to the first man I met, a small, wiry chap with only a few wisps of hair.

"Would you like to join the choir?" he asked me.

I said I would, and he asked whether I was prepared to audition.

"Yes," I said, "though I have no instrument."

"I will play the piano," he said, and he seated himself at a disreputable-looking instrument along the far wall.

He began, but I did not recognize any of the tunes. Finally, I told him that I would sing a couple of songs, and he could pick up the tunes. I sang "The Derby Ram" and "Sweet Betsy from Pike." When I finished there was silence in the room, then applause.

"Wonderful singing," the man said, "but it appears that your religious training is sadly lacking. Never mind. We can fix that."

I turned the subject to the inspector who had been in New Iceland, and asked if anyone there knew his name and where he lived.

"What sort of inspector was he?" one of the men asked. "Was he a fish inspector?"

It had never occurred to me to ask what sort of inspector he had been, but I reasoned that he was most likely inspecting fish and fishermen.

"Not necessarily," someone interjected. "He may have been a school inspector or a licence inspector for trappers, or even a safety inspector. There is no end to the things which can be inspected."

"But if he was an Icelander, then he must have been someone of importance, because not many Icelanders get to be inspectors," another added. The conversation soon turned into a political argument about whether Icelanders did or did not get their just deserts in this new country. It was a small step from politics to religion, and I was asked whether in New Iceland I was a follower of the Pallsmen or the Jonsmen. I knew that there was a considerable argument in New Iceland about the followers of the two preachers, but I had never quite understood the distinction. My father claimed to be a free thinker, and so outside the argument.

The small man with the few wisps of hair explained that the followers of Pall Thorlakson followed the teaching of the Missouri Synod of the Lutheran Church while the followers of Jon Bjarnason followed the teachings of the Icelandic Lutheran church.

The discussion became increasingly heated, and soon there were loud voices and shouts. I was asked to declare myself then and there. Since I knew nothing of what each side represented I took my father's route and declared myself a free thinker.

"It won't do," the wispy man insisted. "This is a church choir, and you cannot be a member unless you adhere to the true church."

"Which is the church of the Jonsmen," someone added.

"Only the followers of Pall will enter heaven," said another, "and there will be no free thinkers in that place."

I slipped out the door and started for home. I knew that when the subject turned to religion and the disputants were Icelanders, there would be no agreement. I had walked only a few steps when I felt an arm on my shoulder. An elderly woman raised her hand to indicate I should be silent, then she said, "His name is Gudmundur Palsson. He has a daughter named Lara, but no wife. He is very wealthy and very dangerous. You would be best to forget about him, whatever it is you want."

"Where does he live?" I asked.

"He lives in a mansion on Broadway. But you must not think of going to his house.

"Why?" I asked. "What might he do?"

"I have already spoken too much," the woman said and she turned back to the hall we had just left. I was happy. I had the first real lead I had found, and though the old woman's warnings were a little frightening, I was sure that they need not prevent my quest.

I returned to the house where Flora worked, and played my guitar and sang for a couple of hours. It was a slow day, and there was only the doctor and one other man drinking in the waiting room, but a half-dozen of the girls were there. They were dressed as usual in nightgowns, but since it was a chilly night, several of them wore slippers and sweaters. I took out my mouth organ and played some tunes on it. The girls were quite excited by this new instrument and they kept singing tunes they remembered from their childhoods and asking me to play the melodies. I played for them and they began to join in singing. A bit later, Minnie herself arrived.

"I think there has been enough singing, girls," she said. "Time for your beauty sleep. Tomorrow will be a busy day. The extra gang from the railway will be in town, and you will have your work cut out for you."

When they left she motioned me to join her in the room she used as an office. The only other person in the waiting room by then was the doctor, and he lay passed out on a sofa. She closed the door to the office and told me that I was not to sing nostalgic songs that would make the girls sad. It was hard enough to keep them working without their getting sad about childhoods and running home. "Happy songs," she said. "No matter what they ask you to play, you will only play and sing happy songs. This is a happy house, and I intend to keep it that way." I nodded agreement, and she waved me out of the door.

I was up bright and early the next day and I found myself on Broadway in a light rain. There were many mansions on that street, and though I had crossed it many times, I had never before walked its entire length. The houses were much larger than any house I had ever entered. Some of the houses had turrets and towers like medieval castles, and many were three stories high. All of them were brand new, and everywhere carpenters were sawing and hammering, and labourers were carrying boards and digging in the ground or carrying bricks to masons who slapped mortar onto walls.

I stopped several people and asked them if they knew which house belonged to Gudmundur Palsson. No one did, but I was sure that if I found it, something in me would know I was there. A horse and cart came down the street at a gallop, and I ducked into an alleyway to avoid being run over. The driver was a tall, stern man with a beard. The young woman on the seat beside him was Lara. She had a bag of books on her lap, and a cape with a hood that nearly hid her face. But that face was burned into my mind, and I had no doubt who it was.

I haunted the street for the rest of that day, hoping I would see her return, but other than getting wet from the rain, I accomplished nothing. As the sky began to darken I stopped at a small café that I had never noticed before. I ordered a cup of coffee and a doughnut, and I began to ponder my next steps. I could come tomorrow at the same time, and perhaps I would see her gallop by once more, but there didn't seem to be much profit in that. I thought that surely others who lived on the street would know someone who owned a mansion, but my inquiries were in vain.

Then someone covered my eyes and breathed a sweet perfume on my face. "Surprise," Lara said, uncovering my eyes and taking the seat across from me. "Did you know it was me?"

"Who else could it have been?" I answered.

"What are you doing here?"

"Looking for you."

"Well, now you have found me, or rather I have found you. What are we to do about this?"

I had no answer. I had been certain that when the opportunity arose I would discover what it was that I wanted to say, and of course I did know that I wanted to declare my undying love for her and promise to wait until we could properly declare that love, but the cold light of the café and the ears of the few other patrons prevented me from speech.

"I wish to speak privately with you," I said.

"You may walk me home," she said and rose from her chair. I was happy that I would discover where she lived. We left the café and walked east toward the forks of the rivers. Before I had finished planning my speech we arrived at a mansion with a round tower at one corner. A light shone from a high window in the tower.

"That is my room," Lara said. "Where the light shines. But it will not be my room for long. We will be leaving before the end of the week."

"Where are you going?" I feared that she might leave Winnipeg or even the entire country and I would never see her again. Her father was a powerful man and could go where he wanted.

"I don't know," she said. "But we will come back here at some time. I am to leave most of my things in my room, so I guess we will have to come back. My father does not discuss his business with me, and so I don't know much."

"He is an inspector," I said. "What does he inspect?"

"I don't know. He has never told me."

"When do you leave?" I asked.

"Before the end of the week." We had reached the walk that led to the door of the mansion.

"Will I see you again before you go?"

"Probably not. My father would not be happy to see you with me. He has plans for my life that do not include the sons of farmers and fishermen. When you saw me this morning, I was being driven to a private school where only the children of the wealthy attend."

"Was that your father driving? He looked bad-tempered."

"No, that was not my father. That is a man hired to take care of me. And he is probably looking for me now. I had better go in."

"I will come tomorrow at the same time to the café. Please meet me there."

"I will if I can. But it might not be possible." Lara turned to the house and began to walk to the door, when suddenly she turned around and ran into my arms. She kissed me a long delightful kiss, and whispered, "That will have to do you for now." And in another moment she had slipped through the door into the house.

I crossed the street, and as I did I met the sullen driver of the cart from the morning. He gave me a hostile glance and walked into the house. I seated myself on a fence where I could watch the light in the tower. After a few minutes I saw Lara approach the window and wave. Then she pulled down the blind, and I made my way to the house where I worked.

Minnie had promised that tonight would be a busy night, and it certainly was. The crew from the extra gang had arrived, and they filled the waiting room. I played a few songs, but they were not interested in music. These were large, powerful men dressed in clothes that badly needed laundering. They laughed loudly and drank whisky directly from the bottles that Minnie sold them. When I started to sing, they shouted at me to stop. They pawed the girls and led them down the hallways to their rooms. I wanted to earn my money, but I didn't want one of the drunken railway men to decide that he could stop the music by breaking my guitar.

Just then, Flora slipped into the room. "Police raid," she said. "Quickly," and she led me through a door that I thought was the door to the closet but led down a short hallway to the outside. "Keep off the streets," she said, and so I made my way home through people's yards and down back lanes. I could see policemen everywhere, and hear their shrill whistles. Hilda's house was brightly lit, and there seemed to be a lot of stir in it. I wondered for a moment whether she too had been raided by the police, but as I entered I heard Icelandic voices, and I guessed that new boarders had arrived from Hecla or Riverton, and that we would soon be crowded. To avoid having to meet these new guests I slipped quietly up the stairs to my room. I leaned the guitar in the corner and went to sleep wondering whether I would have a job tomorrow and whether or not I would meet once more with Lara.

When I awoke the next morning to the snoring of a man in the next bed. I immediately recognized that snore. It was my father. I sat up quietly so as not to awaken him, and saw in a small cradle by the side of the bed, a baby sleeping. The blankets were pink so I surmised it must be a girl, but where in the world would my father have found a baby girl? Such business was mainly my mother's, but there was the undeniable fact that a baby girl was lying in a cradle, her eyes wide open, watching me.

My father's sleep seemed less important than my curiosity, and so I shook him awake. "Ah, Baldur," he said. "It's good to see you. Have you enjoyed your stay in the city?"

"Where were you?" I asked. "What have you been doing for over two months?"

"Well, first I was in Chicago. Lovely city, Chicago. I gave a series of lectures on the Great Northwest. They are curious in Chicago about the Great Northwest, and I played to full houses for a couple of weeks. Then I met a fellow with a dancing bear and we travelled down to Duluth, but some drunk decided that he too should dance with the bear and the bear didn't like that. Bit him on the shoulder. So the police impounded the bear. I worked cutting timber for a while, but it was hard, nasty work, so I went on to Fort William and worked as a stevedore on the docks until I got a letter from your mother asking me to come home. It appears that you will have a new sister."

"And what about this one?" I asked, pointing to the child.

"Ah, Joa," he said. "That's her name. Well that's an interesting story. I found her on the train."

"You found a baby on the train?"

"Well, I didn't just find her lying on the train. She was with her mother and two little brothers. The mother was coming to Winnipeg to find her husband. He had left Toronto to prepare for them to move to Winnipeg, but she hadn't heard from him since they left. She had no money and nowhere to stay, and she couldn't very well look for him with a babe in arms. So I offered to take the child just until she could get back on her feet. We'll all head back to New Iceland tonight."

"Does Mother know about the child?"

"No, but your mother loves children. She won't mind taking care of this one for a few weeks." I wasn't as certain as my father that my mother would be happy at another mouth to feed and another set of diapers to be changed. And then there was the sheer difficulty of getting the baby to New Iceland. You can't just carry a baby while you walk for sixty miles.

"Can we afford to take a coach?" I asked my father. I couldn't see any other way for us to get the baby home.

"Well, actually, I'm a bit short right now. I gave all the money I had to the child's mother so that she would have somewhere to stay and something to eat. You wouldn't happen to have any money, would you?"

"Hilda threatened to put me put on the street if I didn't find some money to pay her for my lodging. So I found myself a job."

"Good boy," my father said. "What did you do?"

"I worked as a shoeshine boy at the railway station."

"A respectable occupation."

"And then I found a job playing music in the waiting room of one of the houses along this street."

My father frowned. "Didn't I forbid you to enter those houses?"

"Yes, but you didn't leave me any money, and so I had to survive. Anyway, I have about thirty dollars. Will that get us home?"

"Yes, certainly. Do you mind giving me the money since I will also have to settle up with Hilda for my own stay." I gave him the money, and I was tempted to tell him about the money from Hannes, but I decided that I would wait a while before I mentioned that. The baby was beginning to fuss, and my father told me to whistle to it. That had always worked with my brothers and my sisters, and it worked again with this baby Joa. She settled down and began to make contented noises. My father went downstairs to talk with Hilda, and left me there with the baby.

"So baby Joa," I said. "What do you intend to do when you grow up?" Joa stared at me with round wide eyes. Apparently she had not given her future much thought. I whistled the "Ode to Joy" for her, and she was soon fast asleep.

"Come on, hurry up," my father shouted from the bottom of the stairway. "The coach will be here in a few minutes and you will get no breakfast if you don't get going."

I loaded up my few belongings and my guitar, and took them down to the hallway at the bottom. Then I went up and picked up the baby and brought it down. It cooed happily, and I kissed it on the head. My father was sitting at the table with a woman who, when I could see her clearly, turned out to be Flora.

"This is Flora," my father said. "I have hired her to come to New

Iceland with us to take care of the baby on the way and to help your mother for the next few weeks."

"How do you do," I said to Flora. I was pretty sure that if my mother knew her profession she would not welcome her into our house.

"Pleased to meet you," Flora said. And we shook hands. I suddenly realized that if we were going to New Iceland, I would not meet with Lara that evening. And she might not forgive me for not being there. Still, I had no choice. Things were taking their own direction, and I had no power in the world.

The trip to New Iceland was uneventful, as such things go. We changed horses in Selkirk and then again at Boundary Creek. I told my father about Hannes, the money, the chess pieces, and the gold watch and fob.

"You did right to take those things," he said. "There was no one here to claim ownership. But you must write his mother and tell her what you have. You may keep what she says you may keep, but the rest must be sent to Iceland."

My father had met Hannes, but did not know him well. "A big silent man," he said. "His people were from Vopnjafjordur in the east, where all the men are big and silent and the women are small and beautiful. He spoke only of returning to Iceland, but apparently death found him before he could go." The baby was very good. Flora fed it milk from a bottle, and hugged it fiercely as if it were her own.

It was dark when we arrived home, but the lamps were lit in all the rooms. My brothers and sisters were all up, waiting for our arrival. My mother immediately took the baby in her arms and went to the room in which she and my father slept. She sang to it and cooed, and made small snuffling noises. My sister set the table and served up a stew my mother had prepared, venison with carrots and turnips, and strong black coffee. The smaller children clambered into my father's arms and sat on his lap as he ate. He fed them spoonfuls of the stew, and they ate as if they had never before been fed. My father was barely visible beneath the clamouring bodies of children, but he seemed happy, though he often called them by the wrong names.

Flora seemed a bit uncomfortable, but our sister spoke almost exclusively to her, telling her about everything that happened in school and evoking names that could not have meant anything to Flora. I was ignored by everyone except my brother, who was interested only in my guitar, which he strummed softly as he sang to himself in a low voice.

My mother finally reappeared with Joa in her arms. She had found new clothes and dressed the baby as if it were going to be christened.

"Be careful," my father said. "The baby is only staying here for a short time until her mother comes for her. Don't get too attached to her."

"The mother is not coming," my mother said. "This is our child from now on. She will be a sister for Maria, who will soon be born."

"How do you know the mother will not come?" Flora asked.

"I have second sight," my mother said. "When I know for certain what the future will bring, I am never wrong."

My mother handed the baby to our sister, who held it tenderly with her hand under its head as if she thought it were fragile and might break. She told Flora that she would sleep in the bed with my sister. The baby would sleep with her and my father until a cradle could be unearthed. My bed had been given to my brothers, and I would sleep on the chesterfield until further notice.

Not only had my bed been given away, but apparently everything I had owned had been divided up among my brothers so that I owned nothing in this world. Not that I had much to begin with. A few small stuffed animals, some books with pictures in them, a pocket knife, a silver necklace given me by the uncle who had died and gone to join the people on the roof. Not only were my belongings gone, they had vanished entirely and none of my brothers had any idea of where they might have gone.

"Lost," they said. "All those things are lost."

My mother had not yet spoken to my father. Now she sent everyone to bed. Then she spoke to him for a long time in a whisper that could be heard but not understood. The chesterfield was uncomfortable. I must have grown taller, because I was too long for it, and my feet hung over the end. There was a loose spring in one of the cushions, and if I rolled on it, it stuck me sharply. I was glad when morning arrived.

My mother sent Flora to school with our sister. She seemed prepared to accept Flora as another child in the way she had accepted Joa. I too went to school, but after a half a day, I was certain that I would not stay there long. My English was so good now that the teacher, though she was English herself, said that she could no longer teach me the language. At noon I returned home, where my father and mother were talking intently. My father was poring over the deed to the farm I had got from Hannes.

"This is my uncle's farm," my father said. "He claimed it because it was abandoned. He has farmed it for five years now, but whoever has this deed could make him leave."

"You have the deed," I reminded my father. "Do you want to make him leave?"

"No, of course not. But he will sleep better if we give him the deed. You must write to Hannes's mother immediately so that we can make the matter clear." I had already written the letter, but had not yet received a reply.

We had no money at all to buy food with. My father had given it all to the mother of Joa. He decided that we could take the money from Hannes as a loan until we could earn enough money to pay him back. Or, since Hannes had no need for money where he was, we could pay back his heirs. I knew then that I could never stay home for any length of time. I would have to go to Winnipeg and find another house where I could entertain the customers and make enough money to pay for food for the family. That is the problem for the first-born. The family must survive, and the first-born bears as much responsibility as the parents.

I needed time to think clearly. A lot had happened in the last few days, and I had to make sense of it. I went for a walk, and soon found myself at the cemetery where the people from the roof slept. I began to whistle to them, not the "Ode to Joy," but happier songs.

When I had finished whistling, I went down on my knees to listen for the voices of the dead. At first, everything was silent. Then I heard a rush of voices like leaves rustling in the wind. I couldn't make out any individual voice, but the melancholy music was inescapable. I took out my mouth organ from my pocket and began to play "Buffalo Gals." Then I listened again. The voices were still indistinct, but they didn't seem as unhappy as they had been. I thought that if I came every day for a week or two, they might speak directly to me.

That evening when Flora came home from school, she was in an ecstatic mood. She had enjoyed every minute of the day. The teacher had been kind to her and had commended her on her excellent penmanship. She had met several other girls, and two of the boys had offered to walk home with her. She had refused and had walked with our sister and a girl named Wilma, who I had never seen before.

The baby was a remarkably good baby, my mother said. She hardly ever cried, and she could smile and laugh. My mother thought she was about two months old. My father had never thought to find out the baby's age. He still believed that the mother would soon come and get the child, even though my mother told him to forget about that idea. My brother was entranced by the chess game. He had seen some of the fishermen playing chess, and they had told him the names of the pieces. He carried the set around with him wherever he went, and he began to play with some of the older fishermen. They told him he was a natural chess player, and he was proud of that. He taught me how to move the men, but I could never win a game. It turned out that Flora knew how to play, and was nearly as good as my brother. She often beat him, which infuriated him because he didn't think girls should play chess.

New Iceland had no houses of the sort in Winnipeg, and so I could not get a job. I still had my shoeshining kit, but the fishermen of New Iceland had little need for shiny shoes. I brooded around the house and spent my afternoons visiting with the dead, but though they came maddeningly close to telling me things, there were too many of them, and I could not make sense of their words. My mother did not want me lying on the chesterfield in the house or practising my guitar. She spoke to my father, and one day he came home and told me that I had a job. I would work at the fishery building, filleting pickerel and saugers and sunfish. I would start at seven in the morning and work until five in the afternoon.

The work was hard. The man to my left headlessed the fish, throwing the heads into a barrel. I cut off the fillets and passed them on to the man on my right, who cut the fillets from the skin and tossed them into a pan. Every few minutes, a woman would come by and take the fillets to another table where she would wrap them in waxed paper and tie string around the package. The packages all weighed one pound, though the woman had no scale and made her decision about how many fillets to include by eying them. Filleting was hard on the back. The only way I could get a moment to stretch was to go so fast that the fish piled up on the table of the man to my right. Then he would have to stop, and I could stretch. The problem was that the man to my right did not want me to go so fast, and the man to my left was always trying to overwhelm me with his speed.

Time passes quickly when you must work nearly every hour of the day. I cannot tell you now whether I worked there for months or years, but I felt that I had been given a stiff jail sentence and hard labour at that.

Then one day we were all called to the office. The foreman told us that today we would have to be especially careful, because the inspector was coming to visit.

"Is this the same inspector who comes out in a boat and checks our nets?" I asked.

"No," the foreman answered. "This is a different kind of inspector. His job is to see that things are being done right. He will be inspecting several different businesses and stores."

"What is his name?"

"His name is none of your business. But he is Gudmundur Palsson from Winnipeg."

So I would finally meet Lara's father. I imagined he would be a large man, dark and brooding and bad-tempered. I thought that he would be a more powerful version of the man who had driven Lara in the cart in Winnipeg. When he arrived, I was surprised. He was a medium-sized man, with blond hair and an elegant grey suit. He was much younger than I had expected. He carried a leather case with papers in it, and he took out his pencil and made notes. He talked in a soft and gentle voice to all the workers. When my turn arrived, he said, "You are Baldur Arnason?"

"Yes."

"You are the one who can whistle and play the mouth organ and the guitar?"

"Yes."

"Do you like this work?"

"No."

"What would you like to do?"

I was surprised to find that he really seemed interested.

"I would like to play music for my living. But there is not much call for music in New Iceland."

He wrote something on a piece of paper and passed it to me, then moved on to the woman who wrapped the fish. I read the note quickly and then put it into my pocket. The note said, "Meet me after work at the town office. I have a proposition I think might interest you."

The rest of the day passed slowly as I wondered what that proposition might be. I had grandiose fantasies about being taken to Winnipeg to live in the same house as Lara, but then I thought that I might be sent somewhere so that I would never see her again. I welcomed the coming dusk at the end of the day.

Gudmundur Palsson was waiting for me when I arrived at the town office. Dusk had settled in and the office was lit by a single lamp. Gudmundur, who had looked gentle and benign in the morning light, seemed monstrous and sardonic in the flickering glow of the lamp.

"Come in," he said. "Take a seat. Make yourself comfortable." The two chairs in the office were both wooden and crudely made. They did not seem intended to make anyone comfortable. "I hear that you are an excellent musician," he went on. "A natural musician, I have been told."

I couldn't imagine who might have told him this except for the guests at the house where Flora had lately been employed, and they didn't seem like the sorts of people who would find themselves in the company of Gudmundur Palsson.

"I have some facility with music," I said, "but I am entirely self-taught. I can only render familiar songs and a few Icelandic ballads."

"Excellent," he said. "That is precisely what I want. An untutored Icelander who can provide sweet music in both Icelandic and English, and who is without pretensions. I have a proposition for you. A couple of months from now, I will be hosting a dinner for some of the most important people in the country. I would like to hire you to perform for about forty minutes, singing in both languages. You will have to be formally dressed, but don't worry, we will provide your costume. And of course you will have to come to Winnipeg at least a week before the concert in order to rehearse and to meet with my people to determine the songs you will present."

"I don't have much money," I told Lara's father. "It is difficult for me to leave my job and go to Winnipeg. Many people would like my job, and when I returned I would find myself without employment."

"Don't worry about that. You will be paid more than you could earn in a season of filleting fish. And of course all your expenses will be covered. I have already spoken to your employer who will not expect you to come to work for at least a month. And if you do a particularly good job, then you may have your dream of living by your music."

I could scarcely comprehend all he had told me. I would be performing for some very important people, and I would receive a salary that would certainly be more than I had ever received before. I would be able to help pay for the food and lodging of my brothers and sisters and the others who lived in our family's house. My father had added two to that number, and the swelling of my mother's belly showed that she, too, was willing to do her share to see that no bed in that house was unfilled.

Gudmundur Palsson told me that his man Gregory would come to me tomorrow with papers to sign, and an advance on my salary. Then he turned down the lamp so the room was in darkness. I was seated near the door, so I simply stood up, opened the door, and slipped out into darkness and lightly falling snow.

Our house was in its usual chaos. Children were playing games, some of which involved a good deal of shouting and running around the room. Flora and my brother were playing chess. My father was writing a letter and my mother was washing the baby. I asked if I could speak to them about something important. They agreed, but scheduled our conference for a couple of hours later when most of the children would be in bed. There was some stew in a pot on the stove and I ate that with a slice of brown bread my mother had made that morning. Then I joined my father in letter writing at the table. I felt that I must get in touch with Hannes's mother as soon as possible. We had possessions that were not ours, and it was my duty to keep the family name honest.

My brother had a name. He was Geiri, but our father always called him "the brother." He referred to the other brothers as "the little boys." He called Asta and me by name, but the other girls were "the little girls," as if he found it too much effort to actually remember their names.

After the children had gone to bed and my brother and our sister had joined Flora in a three-handed card game, I explained Gudmundur Palsson's proposition.

My mother was against it. "I do not trust him," she said. "He is a powerful man, and ordinary people who get involved with powerful folk usually live to rue the day."

My father was all for it, especially since I intended to provide money for the family. "Baldur has lived in the city. He knows the risks," he told my mother. "And he will be home before Christmas, and we can see how the land lies then."

The next morning, I did not go to work as I had been instructed. Instead, I went to the graveyard to consult with the dead. I thought that under the cover of the new snow, they might be less voluble, and I might be able to hear individual voices. I began by playing some songs for them on my mouth organ. I waited a couple of minutes, then I said, "Gudmundur Palsson has offered me a proposition. He wants me to go to Winnipeg and sing at a gathering of important people. What should I do?"

"You should go," said a voice that was not a voice from the dead. I turned and Lara stood behind me, dressed in a parka with a fur-lined hood. "It is a wonderful opportunity," she said.

"Did you have something to do with this?" I asked.

"Only a little. My father described exactly what he wanted in an entertainer, and he described you. I only put him on your trail, and he did the rest by himself."

"I am to meet with Gregory," I told her.

"Yes. Gregory. The man whose job it is to protect me. He does many things for my father."

"Will I see you when I come to Winnipeg?"

"We will find out then. But poor Gregory is out looking for me now. I make his life miserable by slipping away." She walked over to me and kissed me slowly and deliberately, then ran into the bush on the other side of the graveyard and disappeared.

Gregory arrived as scheduled, just a few minutes before noon. He was dressed in a black overcoat and wore a red scarf and a fur hat that made him look like an illustration of a Russian prince I had once seen in a book. He handed me fifty dollars, which was more than I had expected to get for the entire trip to Winnipeg and the performance combined. He also gave me a list of songs that I was to be sure to learn before I arrived in Winnipeg. I tried to engage him in conversation about how long he was staying and when he would return to Winnipeg. He avoided all questions and simply said goodbye and left.

I didn't tell my father and mother about the money I had been given, reasoning that given all the needs and desires of the family, it would all be spent before I could leave, and I would have to walk to Winnipeg. Instead, I hid it in my bag in a small box that said Copenhagen on it, and hoped that my brothers and my sister would not open it even if they raided my bag. Then I walked around the streets of Gimli as I had walked the streets of Winnipeg looking for Lara. She was nowhere to be found, and when I went to the town hall to ask after the whereabouts of Gudmundur Palsson, I was told that he had left, and no, they did not know where he was going.

I was now faced with the difficult problem of finding a place to practise. It was impossible to do anything at home. Somehow, it was now understood that I was a guest in the house, and that I would soon be leaving. I had no bed and certainly no bedroom. However beautiful the music I played, the rest of the family did not wish to hear it while they were about their own affairs.

The problem was solved in an odd way. Magnus Thorkelsson,

who owned the general store with his brother Valdi, was looking for someone to be a night watchman, not because they feared burglars—there were no burglars in New Iceland—but because they feared their merchandise would freeze unless there was fire in the store throughout the night, or else the store would burn to the ground if there were no one watching the fire.

There was a small room at the back of the store where I slept during the day, and I practised my music during the night. Every three hours I would add wood to the stove, poplar sticks that burned fast but did not give much heat. The store had everything anyone could reasonably want in it. It had bags of flour, sugar and salt. It had dried fruit and vegetables. It sold tonic and medicine, dishes and cutlery, cloth by the yard and yarn and knitting needles and clothing, including stockings and mitts and underwear. The walls were lined with axes and shovels and picks and hoes. Harnesses hung from the rafters, halters and traces and yokes and saddles. The smell of leather mixed with the smell of food, and it was a heady mixture.

I was there for only three weeks, but for months after that, smells became associated with the songs I was playing, and I could not sing "Sweet Betsy from Pike" without smelling pickles in brine. "Greensleeves" smelled of polished leather and "Gypsy Boy" smelled like soap. I developed a small following of younger boys and girls whose parents didn't send them to bed. They would gather by the south window, the one with the display of children's toys, and beg me to let them in. I had been expressly forbidden to allow anyone in, and so I watched their pale faces, noses pressed against the glass, and thought about myself at that age. I had never been permitted to go out by myself late at night and I had envied those who did. I no longer envied them. They seemed cold and lonely and not very happy.

I realized as it came time to go to Winnipeg that I had not been told the exact date I was to arrive, or where I was to stay when I arrived in the city. I decided to arrive a few days early and stay at

Hilda's place. I thought I would visit Minnie and see the doctor and remake acquaintances. I thought often of Johnny Ashdown, and I thought I would visit with him. I had plenty of money, and I looked forward to spending some of it.

My brother took over my job at the Thorkelssons' general store. He went to school during the day, and he played chess with Valdi Thorkelsson for a couple of hours just after the store closed. He took catnaps, and kept the store from burning down. I spoke to him shortly before I left for Winnipeg. He told me that the mayor's son had fallen in love with Flora. My brother was jealous, though he claimed that he had no interest in Flora other than as a chess partner.

"What does Flora think?" I asked.

"She is pleased at the attention, but she says that she cannot return his affection. She said she has a terrible secret, and that she can never tell anyone because everyone would hate her if she did. Do you know what this terrible secret is?"

I had an idea that it had to do with her employment at Minnie's house, but it was a secret that I did not want to share even with my brother. I told him I didn't know, but everyone in the world had secrets that they didn't want other people to know.

"Do you have a secret?" he asked.

"Yes, but I will tell no one. And I won't ask you your secret." He blushed at that and agreed that some secrets should stay secrets.

One other thing happened. I received a letter from Iceland. The writer of that letter told me that Hannes's mother had died heartbroken at the news of his death. She had no living relatives, and I was instructed to dispose of his belongings in the way I thought best.

I said goodbye to the family and caught the coach to Winnipeg. Just as we were about to leave, Flora ran up with a letter she wanted me to deliver to Minnie. I put the letter in my pocket and forgot about it. There were two other people on the coach, a fisherman named Helgi, whom I knew slightly, and a young woman named Inga, the daughter of the mayor whom I remembered only as a child.

Helgi was on his way to visit his brother and Inga was going to a private school in Winnipeg. She was a pretty girl with blonde hair and blue eyes. She was very interested in Flora. I told her only that Flora had been hired to help with the baby that Father had found on the train and the new baby that was scheduled to arrive in the near future.

Inga was chatty and eager to find out about the city. She had never been there, and imagined it to be much more exciting than it really was. So the time passed quickly, and before I was prepared for it, we were in the outskirts. Inga was amazed by the size of the buildings. Her grandmother was to meet us at the railway station, which was the final stop for the coach.

When we arrived at the station, I said goodbye to my fellow passengers and walked into the rotunda. There were shoeshine boys at all three stations, but I did not recognize any of them. People were milling about. The train from the east had just arrived, and the arrival area was full. I stood watching for a minute and was just about to go out the door and onto Main Street when I saw a familiar face. Johnny Ashdown was walking toward me, dressed in a dark blue suit with a pale blue tie and white scarf. He carried an overcoat on his arm, and a golden watch fob gleamed at his waist. He was hardly recognizable as the shoeshine boy he had been, and he seemed much older.

"Baldur," he called out. "Good to see you. Where have you been?"

"Gimli," I told him. "Visiting with my family. And you?"

"I am just back from Toronto. Business. I am now in the real estate business. You will remember the property I wanted to buy?" Well, I won some money playing poker, and I put a down payment on the property. The bankers refused to pay what I asked, so I went to Toronto and I have sold it for three times what I had asked the bankers."

"Have you time for a coffee?" I asked.

"No, not now, but how about lunch tomorrow? That little café on Main Street." That was where we had talked the first day of my career as a shoeshine boy.

"Great," I said. "Noon it is." Johnny walked out the door to a coach that was waiting for him. There was a woman in the coach but I could not make out her face.

I was just about to leave myself, when I heard a woman crying. Two men were talking to her, but I could see that she did not want to go with them. I walked over to see what was happening, and found that the crying girl was Inga. I called out her name, and the two men vanished immediately.

"What's wrong?" I asked.

"My grandmother did not come. I was looking all around for her and these men came up and offered to find me a place to stay. I know enough not to go off with strange men, but they were persistent. You probably saved me."

"Well, let's try to find your grandmother," I said, but there was no grandmother to be found after looking around the entire station. I asked for her grandmother's address, and said I would accompany her there.

"It's here in my bag," she said, but when she looked into her bag, her purse with the address and all her money was gone.

"It must have been those men," I told her. "This is not Gimli. There are thieves and desperate people everywhere and you must be careful." I could think of nothing to do but to take her to Hilda's, and she really had no option other than to accept my offer. We set off walking, and in about a half hour we were at Hilda's.

Hilda told me that my room was reserved, but there was no other room available. So many people had arrived in the last few days that there was no room anywhere in the city. I told her that Inga could have my bed and I would sleep in Hannes's bed. Hilda was reluctant, and Inga even more reluctant, to make these arrangements, but in the end there was no other possibility other than sending Inga out into the cold, and so we took our bags up to the room. I put the guitar carefully in the corner and unpacked. Hilda waited at the door until I paid her in advance for the room. "Tomorrow we will find your grandmother," I told Inga. "But tonight you must sleep. You will be perfectly safe here." There was a knock at the door and Hilda arrived with coffee and biscuits. She had never done this in all the time I had stayed there alone, and so I assumed that she had something she wanted to say to me.

"What is Inga's grandmother's name?" she asked.

Inga told her, "Signy Torfadottir, widow of Jon Gislason the printer."

"I think I know who she is," Hilda said. "I will find the address first thing in the morning and I will take you there myself. And you," she said, indicating that she was speaking to me, "you take as good care of her as if she were your sister."

I agreed I would do just that. She slept fully clothed, and I felt better when she began to snore a gentle soft music. Then I climbed into my own bed and fell into a deep sleep. At some point in the night I awoke to a sweet perfume and hair tickling my face. Inga had climbed into bed with me. I put my arm around her and she murmured something, but she did not awake. A little later I could hear Hilda scrambling around in the kitchen, making breakfast.

When I awoke I was alone in the room. I made my way downstairs and found Inga and Hilda together in the kitchen. Hilda had found Inga's grandmother, who had been taken to the hospital. The doctors did not know what was wrong with her, but she would have to stay there for at least a week. They had visited her, and she had given Inga a key to her house, but Inga was afraid to stay there alone. Would I be willing to stay with Inga at her grandmother's until the grandmother came home or someone from Gimli came to take care of her? I agreed, of course, but I was worried that my life was sufficiently complicated that I didn't need Inga to complicate it further.

I had slept late, and it was nearly time for me to meet with Johnny. I told Inga that I would be back by mid-afternoon to take her to her grandmother's house. I also agreed to take her to the hospital to visit her grandmother.

I was a few minutes late arriving at the café, and Johnny was already there. Again, he was dressed in a suit and was smoking a small cigar. We ordered lunch, liver and onions with bread and coffee. I told Johnny about Inga and my dilemma about having to take care of her.

"How old is she?" he asked. I guessed that she was probably sixteen.

"And what does she look like?" Inga was beautiful, there was no denying that, yet I had not thought of her beauty until asked.

"She is beautiful," I told Johnny. "She is blond with blue eyes and wonderful skin."

"Then you have no problem. She is of marriageable age, and she must be attracted to you or she would not have contrived to have you stay alone with her. You do not have a dilemma. You have an opportunity."

I reminded Johnny that I was already in love, and even if I wasn't, I would not take advantage of a young woman. He asked whether I had taken advantage of Flora, and I told him that of course I had not.

"You are either very naïve or a saint," Johnny replied.

I tried to change the subject, and Johnny seemed willing to go along with me. I asked about his new career in real estate.

"My career is not in real estate," he answered. "My career is in making money. Already this morning I have bought a large number of lots just at the edge of the city. The police have raided the brothels, and the citizens want them moved out of sight. I intend to approach each of the madams and sell them lots. Then I will build houses for them, and provide regular delivery of beer and whisky. With the profits from this, I will build the biggest warehouse in the city, and start a number of food stores that I will supply from the warehouses. In five years, I will be the richest man in the province."

I believed everything he said. He was so confident and so full of ideas that I had no doubt he would succeed. He offered me a cigar, but

I remembered my adventure with Hannes's snuff, and so I declined. Johnny called for the bill and gave the waitress a large tip. She smiled and curtseyed, and Johnny winked at her. Then when we were leaving the café, she rushed up to us and, blushing, handed Johnny a note. He read it, nodded his head to her, and we left. I was curious about the note, but I didn't ask him about it.

After we had walked together for about a block, he said, "That note was an invitation to meet the waitress when her shift is over. The tip I gave was an investment. I will meet her and take her out for dinner. Perhaps some day I will need her, and she will be under an obligation to me. It is important to make alliances, even unlikely ones. You never know what the world will deliver you." We shook hands and parted.

Inga's grandmother lived in a large house near the river. It was not as grand as Gudmundur Palsson's house, but it was only a short distance from it, and it was nearly as grand. The walls were covered with paintings of Icelandic scenes, and there were many elegant mirrors and chandeliers. The floors were oak, with several Persian carpets.

Inga showed me to a room that she said would be mine for as long as I stayed. She thanked me for my generosity, and vowed that her father would repay me handsomely. I of course would not hear of repayment. I had picked up my guitar from Hilda's when I went to get Inga. I asked whether she would mind if I practised.

"Please do," she said. "I love music, though most of my family do not." I ran through my repertoire, and when I had finished she clapped her hands loudly. I bowed a deep bow, a kind of mocking rehearsal for the bow I would have to make after my performance.

It was starting to get dark when we set out for the hospital. A chilly wind had come up and Inga was not dressed for it. I put my arm around her to keep her from the wind, and we arrived at the hospital arm in arm. The nurse informed us that her grandmother was worse. The doctor who was taking care of her was sick himself, and they had been unable to find another. Inga broke into tears, and she was weeping copiously when we entered her grandmother's room. I saw an old woman, so thin she seemed fragile. She was sleeping, but every few minutes she cried out in pain.

"We have to do something," Inga said. "Can't we find another doctor?"

I remembered then the doctor who had attended Hannes.

"Wait here," I told Inga. "I have an idea. I will be right back." I headed for Minnie's house, certain that the doctor would be there if he had not been arrested in the police raid. The lights in the house were ablaze when I arrived.

Minnie met me at the door, and I only remembered then the letter from Flora. It was still in my pocket. I gave it to her and asked for the doctor. She opened the note, glanced at it, and said, "Doctor Smith no longer comes here every night. He has stopped drinking and has gone back to being a doctor. But you are in luck. One of the girls is sick, and he has just arrived to care for her. I'll tell him you are here."

The doctor arrived a few minutes later. He seemed filled with energy and he welcomed me. "There you are, young fellow. I am in your debt. If you and Flora had not shown me the back way out from this house, I would have been hauled off by the police as a common criminal." I had not realized that the doctor had followed us out, but I hoped his gratitude would extend to caring for Inga's grandmother,

I told him my story in as few words as possible and he agreed to come immediately. When we got to the hospital, the nurse informed us Inga's grandmother was worse. She expected her to die any minute. The doctor took a vial out of his black bag and poured some liquid into a spoon and forced it between her teeth. After a few minutes she stopped crying out and fell into a deep sleep.

"She'll be fine tonight," the doctor said. "She is not out of danger yet, but I will call on her early in the morning. Now there's no need to sit at her bedside all the night. There is nothing you can do. Go home and get some sleep so that you can visit her tomorrow."

Inga had stopped weeping. She gazed at the doctor as if he were himself a miracle. The doctor spoke with the nurse, giving her instructions that meant nothing to me. We waited for him at the door, and then the three of us walked out into the winter night.

Inga invited the doctor to join us at her grandmother's house for a cup of coffee. The doctor agreed, and we walked back through a gentle snowfall. It turned out that the doctor lived only a short distance from Inga's grandmother. We passed by his place on our way, a rather small brick house with many windows and a door that had been painted red.

The doctor did not stay long. He said that he was still wrestling with his demons, and that was best done at home. Before he left, however, a young boy knocked at the door and asked for me. He handed me a note that read, "Please present yourself at the front door of Gudmundur Palsson's house at exactly nine-fifteen tomorrow." The signature was a scrawl that I could not make out. I explained that I would be unable to accompany Inga to the hospital in the morning. The doctor volunteered to pick Inga up on his way to the hospital at eight o'clock, and then he left us in an awkward silence.

I picked up my guitar and began to strum some arbitrary chords. Inga sat down at the piano, and to my surprise played the Icelandic song "Á Sprengisandi" with its rollicking rhythm that always reminded me of the beat of horse's hoofs. She sang in a small sweet voice and I joined in with her. We didn't have many songs in common, but I taught her "The Golden Vanity" and she taught me an Icelandic song about a little boy lost in the mountains while looking for sheep. He mistakes the roar of the river for his father's voice and he is carried away and drowned. It is a sad song, but she didn't know its name, only that her father often sang it when he drank whisky. She said it was fortunate that he seldom drank, because every time she heard the

song she was made terribly sad. I replied that "The Golden Vanity"
was also sad, and it was also about a young boy who drowned.

Then we turned off the lamps and went each to our own room.
I found it hard to sleep, wondering about what I would discover
tomorrow, and even more hoping I might get a chance to talk to
Lara. I heard Inga walking around the house several times during
the night, but she made no attempt to talk to me, and I kept my own
silence.

I awoke the next morning to hear Inga bidding me goodbye, and the doctor's loud voice laughing in the hallway. I dressed quickly and ate some porridge Inga had set out for me. It was still too early to go to the house of Gudmundur Palsson, so I sat waiting for the clock to tick off the minutes until I could go. Finally, after what seemed a long time, the clock struck nine and I headed out. Even then, when I checked Hannes's golden watch in my pocket, I was five minutes early and had to stand outside on the sidewalk. I waited until the watch said precisely nine-fifteen, and then I climbed the stairs and knocked on the door.

The door swung open, and there was Lara, still dressed in her nightgown. "Hush," she said and touched her finger to her lips. She led me to a small sitting room just off the main entrance. "You will meet with Gregory in fifteen minutes. He will give you instructions about what is expected of you." She took a seat across from me and put her feet up on a small table.

"Well," she said, "tell me everything."

I had no idea where to start, so I began with the coach ride to Winnipeg. I told her of Inga and her unfortunate grandmother, and the doctor and the hospital.

"I see you are a man who has great adventures," she said. "Tell me more about Inga. Is she very beautiful?"

"She is somewhat pretty," I replied.

"And now you are living with her?"

"Only for a few days until her people arrive from New Iceland."

"I had expected to break your heart," she said. "I did not expect you to break mine. But there it is. Nothing is certain in this world."

"There is nothing between us. She is merely a young girl in distress whose grandmother is probably dying in the hospital as we speak. I love only you, and it is almost certain that I will continue to go on loving you. You will have plenty of time to break my heart."

"Good," she said. "I am reassured. Now it is time for you to meet with Gregory." She motioned for me to follow, and we went up a flight of stairs to a large room with a desk and more books than I had ever seen gathered in one place.

Gregory was seated at the desk, and a small man with a goatee sat on a chair facing the desk. There was one other chair, and Gregory motioned me to take it. I sat down and Gregory continued to speak to the other man in a language I did not recognize but thought might be French. After a few moments, he apologized and informed me that Monsieur Dorge was from Montreal, and that he would accompany me on the piano at our little entertainment.

"Pleased to meet you," I said to Monsieur Dorge, and he answered, "No, no, nothing at all. I will be pleased to work with you." And he stood and made a slight bow.

Gregory took some papers out of the drawer of the desk and asked me to sign them. I did so without reading them, and he gave me an envelope with some more money in it and a set of keys.

"The keys are to this house through the back entrance. You will have a room to stay in, though I gather you have found your own living arrangements," he said, his voice rising as if he had asked a question.

"Only for a couple of days. But how did you know where I was?"

"Your friend Hilda is quite talkative. When we could not find you in Gimli, we asked people who directed us to her and she was very helpful. But you will stay here for a while?"

"Yes," I said. "I will be here in a couple of days."

"You will rehearse with Monsieur Dorge in the music room. And you had better make arrangements to do so now. There is not much time left before the performance." He stood up from his chair and left the room without saying goodbye.

Monsieur Dorge informed me his name was Gerard, and I was to address him as such. Then he led me down a long hallway to a room with a piano and an organ and a range of other instruments. About a dozen chairs were arranged in a semicircle around the piano. And high windows looked over the street. The heavy purple curtains were not drawn. Gerard opened the seat of the piano and drew out several sheets of music and handed them to me. I told him I did not read music.

"I see," he said. "That makes everything more difficult. But you have a good memory? You can learn everything by heart?"

I assured him I would do my part. He sat down at the piano and began to play some simple songs. I sang them with him, all the verses of each song, and he seemed pleased.

"Tomorrow you will bring your guitar," he said. "We will meet here at two in the afternoon." He walked off down the hallway, leaving me to wonder how I would get out of the house. As soon as he was gone, Lara appeared to escort me to the door. She was still wearing her nightgown. She led me to the rear door, kissed me on the cheek and pushed me out the door.

When I arrived back at Inga's grandmother's house, the doctor was just leaving. "She's doing fine," he said. "She should be home in a couple of days." He put on his coat and went to the door. "I'll see you tomorrow," he told Inga, and he left, pulling the door closed with such strength that it made the mirrors in the hall rattle.

"My father will be here tomorrow," Inga told me. "He sent a message. You will have to find somewhere else to live."

"That's taken care of," I told her. "I will be staying at Gudmundur Palsson's house for the next little while. I am rehearsing with a man named Gerard Dorge who is from Quebec." I described Gerard with his little goatee and his quaint accent. Inga laughed.

"You will make a good pair," she said. "A tiny man, and you are so large." I hadn't thought about my size for quite some time. And I did not think of myself as large, though now when I looked in the mirror I could see I must have grown quite a lot in the last few months. I noticed also that my hair had grown long, and though I had been blond since birth, I was now quite dark. It was lunchtime, but there was nothing in the house for lunch. I offered to take Inga to the little café just down the street, and she agreed.

Over lunch I asked her how much money she had. She had none. I took ten dollars out of the money that Gregory had given me and offered it to her. At first she refused, but then she took it on the agreement that her father would pay me back as soon as he arrived in Winnipeg.

The next day Inga's father did arrive along with her brother. They went to the hospital and brought the grandmother home immediately. She seemed to have recovered miraculously. I met them only for a few minutes when they arrived, and was thanked for all my help. The brother wanted to talk to me about Flora. Where had she lived? Did she have family in Winnipeg? How long would she stay in New Iceland?

I told him that I knew very little about her past. I said that I thought she had come here from the east when she was quite young. I did not tell him about Minnie's place. On the other hand, I knew he would be devastated if he actually found out her history. I felt a few gentle lies would probably be the safest course to follow.

The next few days passed quickly. I rehearsed with Monsieur Dorge, and I roamed through Gudmundur Palsson's house, but I did not see Lara again. Once, I dared to climb up to her room in the tower. Her door was open, but she was not there. Instead, clothes were flung everywhere, the bed was unmade and books lay open on the floor and on her dresser. It was the messiest room I had ever seen. It looked as if she had suddenly been abducted.

Gregory came into the music room a couple of times, but he did not seem interested in the music. He bustled about, looking through the drawers of the desk and making notes in a notebook he carried with him. I wanted to ask him about Lara, but I did not have the courage. I tried to engage him in conversation, hoping I might turn the conversation in a direction where he would have to bring up Lara of his own accord, but he was brusque and not in any mood for idle talk.

Just before he left, he asked Monsieur Dorge and me to meet him the next morning at ten. He would explain all the details of the dinner party at which we would entertain. Then we would have one last rehearsal, and we would perform that very evening. I had not expected this. For some reason I had thought that the performance was a long way off. And it struck me then that when the performance was over, Gudmundur Palsson would have no further need of me, and I would have to consider where I would live and what I would do.

The first thing that I imagined was that I would go back to New Iceland, but it seemed an impossible thing to do. For one thing, my parents had given away my bed, and while it was not a problem to spend a night on the sofa, that was not where I wanted to spend the rest of my life.

I considered my options. My only talent was the production of music, and the only job I could think of other than performing for Gudmundur Palsson was playing for Minnie's clientele. That would keep me alive, but it wasn't a future I looked forward to, and there was the added difficulty of the police who would surely catch me one day or another. The thought of fishing on Lake Winnipeg at thirty below was no more attractive.

I left the house, intending to go to Lara's place, but when I arrived I found that I had walked right past the door, and I did not want to go back. I walked over to Minnie's, where I could see the girls through the window in the blazing lights. I felt I could no longer enter there, nor could I go to Hilda's place. Instead, I wandered down to the railway station. I passed the café where Johnny and I had dined together, and saw through the window that Johnny was there, sitting at the same table at which we had sat before.

I went in, walked over to the table and said hello.

"It's about time," Johnny said. "What kind of friend abandons those who care about him and never visits?"

"I don't know where you live," I reminded him.

"That's true," he said. "Then I forgive you. What have you been up to? Tell me more of the saga of the beautiful Inga."

I told him about the ill grandmother and the arrival of the father and brother. I told him about the doctor, but he seemed to know all about the doctor, so I didn't say more. Then I told him about Gudmundur Palsson and the dinner at which I would entertain the following day. I described Monsieur Dorge and Johnny laughed. Finally, I confessed my fears about what I would do after the performance. Where would I go? What would I do?

"Do you have any money?" he asked.

"Quite enough for the time being, and I am told I will be paid handsomely for the performance, as long as I perform well. Apparently some of the richest and most powerful people in the entire country will be there. I mustn't disappoint them."

Johnny was very interested. "Will you actually meet them or simply perform and disappear?" That question had not occurred to me. I had assumed that I would be introduced to them, that I might even have dinner with them, but I would not have that information before I talked to Gregory the next day.

"Are you willing to risk your money in order to become rich?" Johnny asked. I thought that he had changed the topic, but apparently he had not.

"Yes, of course," I answered, though that option had never before occurred to me."

"Good," Johnny said. "The day after the performance you will meet with me and bring all your money. I have a real estate deal that will make us both a lot richer. But it will also depend on having some influence in high places, and so I want you to cultivate the high and mighty who will attend your performance. The deal will be entirely in your name, but we will share the proceeds."

I asked whether I might know the details of the scheme, but he merely answered, "Trust me. If it doesn't work I will also be back shining shoes. It will work." We shook hands then, and after a few more minutes of conversation in which Johnny informed me that he was considering marriage, we parted.

I walked back towards Gudmundur Palsson's house wondering just what I had done. I had promised all the money I owned to a scheme that I did not understand. I had made myself even more nervous than I had been simply waiting for the performance. And it was beginning to snow again. The lights were on at Inga's grandmother's house, and I walked up the driveway and knocked on the door.

Inga answered. Her father and brother had gone home and left her there to take care of the grandmother. Her brother could not bear to be so long away from Flora. Her father was the mayor and had many meetings to attend.

I asked after the grandmother. She was well, much better than anyone expected. The doctor came every day to visit. Where had I been?

I explained that I had a lot of rehearsing to do, and that the performance would take place the following evening. Then I told her about

Johnny and his offer. I hadn't intended to, but I guess the pressure of having made such a decision made me want some sort of support.

"You are mad," Inga said. "You will risk all your money on some crazy scheme with a man who will not even tell you what the scheme is?" I considered. She was almost certainly right, but I had given my word and we had shaken hands. There was nothing else I could do.

"I have given my word," I said. "A man must honour his word."

"Men are crazy," she answered. I agreed. But there it was. I said goodbye and walked out into the night. She made no attempt to stop me.

The next day I was up bright and early. I had my breakfast and went out for a walk. To my surprise, there was a light in Lara's window. I watched for a while, but there was no movement.

When I returned Gregory was waiting for me in the music room. "You are well rehearsed?" he asked, and I replied that I was as rehearsed as I could be.

"Good, good," he said. "There will be a number of important people here tonight. You will hear some conversation, but I want you to promise that whatever you hear or overhear, you will repeat it to no one." I promised as much, though I didn't imagine state secrets would be discussed in my hearing.

"The premier of the province will be here," Gregory said. "Do you know who is the premier?"

"Tom Greenway," I answered. "He was much in the news over the schools and his banning the use of French. I once shined his shoes at the railway station. He is a big man with a beard."

"And the mayor of Winnipeg?" I had to confess that I did not know who was mayor.

"Andrew Pearson." Even after he told me the name I could remember nothing about him. "There will be a number of local businessmen as well. Dan Sprague, the lumberman; James Ashdown, the hardware man; Nick Bawlf, the grain man; Ted Burrows, the other lumberman; and a few more who you will meet tonight. But the big surprise is that both Lord Stanley, the Governor General, and John Thompson, the new prime minister, will be here. They are here to meet with Greenway to discuss a number of matters, but no one is to know that they are here."

I had heard of Lord Stanley. I had seen pictures of him in the newspapers, a tall man who also sported a beard. But I was unaware of John Thompson. "Isn't Abbott the prime minister?"

"He was until he resigned a short while ago. Now Thompson has taken over. He is something of an unknown quantity. Now, do you have any questions?"

"Why is Gudmundur Palsson hosting this event?"

"Gudmundur is the leader of a group of Icelandic men who are active in real estate. Some important decisions are going to be made in the next few weeks, and they will need some political support. You are going to represent Canadian Icelandic culture, so do your best."

I promised that I would, and he left the room. It struck me then that he had not mentioned any women. Would these men bring their wives with them, or was this only for important men? Would Lara attend?

At five o'clock, the guests began to arrive. I watched from my window as their carriages drew up to the front door and the guests began to enter the house. There were obviously going to be women at the affair. Snow was falling lightly, and it settled on their capes and fancy hats. The horses stamped and their breath made little haloes of steam. I could hear excited talk, though I could not make out any of the words.

Gregory came by and told me to wait for fifteen minutes and then come to the drawing room. I checked the time on Hannes's watch, and waited as it ticked off the minutes. At precisely fifteen minutes, I descended the stairs to the drawing room. About twenty people mingled in the room. Most of them had glasses in their hands. I recognized the premier, but I didn't know many of the others.

Lara suddenly appeared, dressed in a long green gown, the colour of her eyes. She didn't look like the girl I had known, nor the schoolgirl I had recently encountered. She looked like a grown woman, and the men in the room greeted her warmly. Suddenly it became clear to me how hopeless my case was. She fit in perfectly as one of the wealthy and powerful, and I would soon be the clown who entertained them.

She came over to me, made a slight curtsey and said, "I hope you are in fine voice tonight, Baldur. I have been looking forward to hearing you for many weeks now."

I may have blushed. Certainly I felt uncomfortable. "What practice can do has been done," I replied. "I will either be ready or I will not, but it will not be for lack of preparation."

"I am to be the hostess," Lara told me. "My father has asked me to mingle with the guests, so I must do my job." She left me standing there and struck up a conversation with a couple of ladies who were waiting to have their drinks refilled.

I looked around the room to see if there was anyone I recognized. I thought that one of the men had been a member of the Icelandic men's choir, but I could not be sure. I could identify Thomas Greenway, a large man with a large beard. He was explaining why he had named his town Crystal City.

"We are looking for immigrants from Britain, and they are far more likely to choose a place with an attractive name than one with some unpronounceable Indian name." He was speaking to a younger man dressed rather formally with a black bow tie.

The man he was speaking to replied, "Ideally, yes, we want British immigrants, but there are not enough of those to open the west. We are going to have to search more widely. We have our Mennonites and our Icelanders, and both races seem to adapt well. But again, there are few of them. I think ultimately we are going to have to attract Germans and Poles and Slavs. There are hundreds of thousands of peasants who are eking out a miserable living in Ruthenia and Galicia and Bukovenia, but who can farm and who could help develop the prairies. And we are going to need hundreds of thousands of them."

Greenway agreed. "We are going to need a lot of settlers. The next twenty years are going to see this city grow like nothing anyone has ever seen before." I suddenly felt myself more interested in Johnny's plans. The city was going to grow, and anyone who had vision would grow rich along with the city.

There was a sudden scurrying and exclamations at the arrival of two men wearing leather greatcoats and a small pretty woman. I recognized the first as the Governor General. Gregory announced their arrival.

"Ladies and gentlemen. All rise for Lord and Lady Stanley of Preston." There was subdued clapping, and Lord Stanley bowed a sort of half-bow to the assembled company. Gregory went on, "And welcome as well the new Prime Minister of Canada, the Right Honourable John Sparrow David Thompson." Thompson echoed Lord Stanley's bow and the assembly applauded him as well.

Thompson did not look well. His face was pale and he seemed short of breath. Gudmundur Palsson met them and bowed, then called Lara to his side and introduced her. She seemed completely confident, chatted with the men for a few moments, then led Lady Stanley to another group of ladies and introduced her to them. I wandered around the room, trying to hear the various conversations. Nobody paid any attention to me, and I picked up smatterings of information. John Abbott, the previous prime minister, was ill and was not expected to live. That was why he had resigned and made Thompson prime minister. Grover Cleveland, the American president, had made a speech that had rankled Gladstone. Winnipeg was proud of the new electric streetcars that had begun service in September. The Winnipeg Electric Street Railway Company had a thirty-five-year lease, which somebody I did not know thought was far too long.

A couple of men were standing in a corner with Gudmundur Palsson. They were speaking in Icelandic. I moved behind a door where I could hear what they said though they could not see me. There was to be an auction of lots in one week in what they referred to as the west corner. They were going to try to corner the market. All they required was a small down payment for each lot. Then they could sell them all within a short time, and make a large profit. Gudmundur Palsson cautioned them not to mention the scheme to anyone.

I was growing increasingly nervous about the performance, and I was anxious for it to be over, and that I not have it waiting for me. People were filing into the dining room when I finally found Gregory and tried to beg off attending the dinner.

"That is impossible," he said. "All the seating has already been decided. You will have to find your name card on the table and take that seat. Your tablemates would be offended if you decided to abandon them." I had expected a single long table, but there were several tables set, and men dressed in black pants and white shirts were already carrying trays. I found my place and took my seat. I was seated next to Lady Stanley, and that only increased my nervousness.

She turned out to be easy to talk to and after a few pleasantries about the weather, she asked me whether I played hockey. I told her that no, I had tried the game, but I was not skilled. I had never learned to skate well enough to play.

"Nonsense," she said. "Anyone can play for the sport of it. No one expects you to be brilliant. Back in Ottawa on the skating rink at Rideau Hall there is a constant run of hockey games, and some of those playing seem almost totally unable to skate. They do it for the exercise and for the fun." I promised her I would try the sport the next time I had a chance.

"Lord Stanley has just given a cup to be awarded to the top-ranking hockey team in the country," she said. "Perhaps the next time we meet you will be playing for the cup." I was pretty certain that was not going to happen, but I smiled and agreed. Dinner turned out to be an appetizer of smoked goldeye, a fish of which Lady Stanley had never heard, and pickerel fillets with a main course of venison. I ate little for fear I might be unable to sing if I had eaten too much. I could see Lara at another table conversing deeply with a young man, and I felt a rush of jealousy. I made a point of not looking in that direction.

Finally, they brought in dessert, and I made my apologies and went up to the music room. Brandy was being served downstairs, but a number of people, including the Icelanders, had opted not to drink. There had been a group of non-drinking Knights Templar back in New Iceland, and I assumed that there must also be such an institution in Winnipeg.

Finally the rest of the guests arrived and took their seats. Monsieur Dorge sat down at the piano. Gudmundur Palsson introduced me briefly, and talked for a few minutes about the history of the Icelanders both at home and in the New World. Then Monsieur Dorge struck the first notes and I began. I sang "O Gud vors lands," Iceland's Thousand Years, a song that had been written a few years earlier to celebrate the thousand years since the settlement of Iceland. It is a particularly difficult song to sing, but when I was finished, there was general applause, and someone, Lara I think, murmured, "beautiful." I followed the slow, sweet rhythms of the anthem with a lively version of "Á Sprengisandi." The song is a rollicking story of a trip on horseback through the central wastelands of Iceland. I explained it was probably the most popular of all Icelandic songs, and that its rhythms imitated the sound of galloping horses' hoofs. *"Ridum, ridum, og rekum yvir sandinn,"* I began, and by the time I had reached the second verse some of the Icelanders had joined in, including a woman I had not seen before. Again the applause was heartening.

The rest of the concert was easy, and it was over before I was aware of it. I sang "The Derby Ram," because I knew that Lord Stanley had also been named the Earl of Derby, and he applauded louder than anyone else when I was finished.

Several of the men came up after the performance and passed me their cards. I put them in my pocket to look at later. People were complimentary and I was quite pleased with myself. The Icelandic woman whom I had noticed during the performance told me to come to the Lutheran Church on Victor Street any Sunday, and the people there would have an interesting offer to put to me. I tried to answer with as much modesty as I could muster, though I was not feeling particularly modest.

Gregory came by and told me to meet him in the music room tomorrow at ten sharp. And then they were all gone and I was there alone. I wanted to celebrate, to rehearse the events of the day, but there was no one to talk to. I thought I should go out for a walk, and if the lights were on at Inga's house I might stop there for a while. I was on my way down the stairs when Lara caught up with me.

"You did a splendid job," she told me. "Daddy is pleased. The whole evening was a grand success." We were walking down the steps toward the door, so I asked Lara if she wanted to join me for a brief walk. She said no, she could not come even if she wished to, because she was leaving early in the morning for Toronto. Her father wanted her to go to school in the east, and she was leaving on the early train.

"So I will not see you for some time?" I asked.

"I'll be back. I am just going to look at a couple of places. I don't want to go, but we'll see what happens." We had reached the door. She gave me a quick kiss and ran back up the stairs. I walked out into another snowy night. It was cold, but there was no wind. The lights were on at Inga's grandmother's house, so I walked up the stairs and knocked at the door.

Inga answered the door so suddenly that I wondered if she had been waiting for me, and that, it turned out, was the case.

"I was hoping you would come," she said. "How did the concert go?"

"It wasn't really a concert," I said, "just a small performance, but I think it went well. There was plenty of applause, and several people gave me their cards and asked me to call."

"I am full of news," Inga said. "Tomas has asked Flora to marry him. She hasn't given him her answer yet, but don't you think that is wonderful news?" I wasn't so sure it was wonderful. Flora would either have to tell him about her past or live with a secret for the rest of her life. Still, there was nothing I could do about it, so I agreed that it was wonderful.

"And I have been accepted into the Normal School. I will live here with my grandmother while I learn how to be a teacher."

"Do you want to be a teacher?" I asked her.

"Yes, of course."

"You may have to go and teach in a one-room country school, you know. It can be hard work."

"But I love kids, and that's half the battle. I'm sure it will be great. And I have a letter from your father." She passed me a letter that lay on a small table near the door. "I was at Hilda's and she gave this to me."

I opened the letter and stared at my father's scrawling note. He said that I should come home immediately. He had a wonderful opportunity for the two of us to take a dog team to the States, but he could only tell me about it in person. I read it aloud to Inga.

"It sounds mysterious," she said.

"My father has a way of making even the ordinary mysterious. I hope he doesn't want to travel. There is already almost no room at home, and he has a habit of bringing home stray people."

"Do you want to stay the night?" Inga asked. I told her that I had to meet with Gregory early the next morning, and that I would have lunch with Johnny Ashdown, but that I would come by in the evening.

"Promise?"

"Yes." Then, I don't know why I did it, but I took her in my arms and kissed her. She seemed surprised but willing. I left immediately so that I would do nothing more, and I brooded about what I had done until I awoke the next morning.

Gregory was in the music room as he had promised. He gave me an envelope with two hundred dollars in it. It was more money than I had ever had in my possession before.

"Gudmundur Palsson was pleased with your performance. He asks that you make no serious plans until he can talk to you. He has gone east to Toronto with his daughter, but he will be back in about ten days." I asked if he could tell me more about Gudmundur Palsson's plans, but he said he didn't know what they were. He told me I could stay in my room at least until Gudmundur's return.

I met Johnny at noon as we had planned, in the restaurant across from the railway station. He wanted to know everything that had happened at the dinner, and I told him what I could. Gregory had warned me not to talk about what I had heard, but I couldn't think of anything that was more than casual conversation. Johnny, however, could, and he found everything I said interesting. I told him about the Icelanders who were trying to buy up a bunch of land in the west end, and he nodded and said, "I knew something was up but I had no idea who was doing it. I think we might do well to buy some land in the area."

I took out my envelope of money and handed it to him. He counted and said, "This is a good deal more than I expected. Is this all the money you have?" I told him that I had kept twenty dollars, but that I would soon be back at Minnie's playing for the customers unless we made some money soon.

"Don't worry," he said. "We will have a lot of money in a short while. And I'd try to keep away from Minnie's if I were you. You need a clean reputation to do some of the things we're going to need from you in the future. If you run out of money, I will give you some."

I thanked him, and after about an hour's conversation about the railway station, shining shoes and his trips to Toronto, we parted. I headed back towards Gudmundur Palsson's place. I had begun to sweat, though it was a cold day. My head had begun to swim and I had trouble focusing on things. Everything seemed to be doubled, the building, the people and the street signs. I stopped at a bench to rest, and felt myself sinking into sleep. Sometime later, I awoke and found myself terribly cold. I forced myself to get up and start walking, though every step took a huge effort. Finally I found myself in front of Inga's grandmother's house, and I struggled up the path to the door. I knocked at the door, but there was no answer. At last, at last, Inga opened the door and I fell into the room and collapsed on the floor. The room was warm and smelled of spruce boughs. I thought it must soon be Christmas, and that is the last I thought for a long time.

The days that followed are a blur. I had an overwhelming desire to sleep, and someone was always waking me up. Food was spooned into my mouth but it had no taste. I washed, or somebody washed me. I went to the toilet when I was made to go. People spoke to me but I could never remember what they said. Faces appeared to me in flashes, spinning in ever-changing colours like a kaleidoscope. The doctor appeared, as did my father and for one brief second, Hilda. Johnny was there but I only remember his mouth making round movements and I could not understand what he said. Inga was there, but I remembered only her hands on my face. I tried to get up, but I felt that I was drowning in a sea of cotton. I couldn't come to the surface.

Then one morning, I awoke to find myself soaked in sweat. The room, which had been spinning for as long as I could remember, was finally still. The doctor was sitting on a chair by my bed reading a newspaper. I felt I should say something, and so I said, "Good morning."

"Good morning, indeed," he answered. "You are a lucky young man. I almost gave up on you several times, but here you are, apparently determined to survive."

"What was wrong with me?" I asked.

"That's not easy to say. It may have been any of a number of things, or it may even have been several things at once. You have had an extraordinary variety of symptoms, and I hesitate to name any particular disease. If you had been to Africa, I might have guessed malaria. In fact, I consulted Dr. Elizabeth Matheson, who has worked in Africa and has survived malaria herself. She thought it unlikely that you could have contracted the disease in Winnipeg."

"A woman doctor?" I asked. I had never before heard of one.

"Yes, and a good one," he answered. "I have treated you for many different things, and something seems to have worked. You are alive and will probably recover entirely."

"Inga?" I asked.

"Yes, Inga. She is a saint. Without her I don't think we'd be discussing your good luck today. She has nursed you day and night for over two months. You are deeply in her debt."

"Where is she?"

"She has gone to the hospital. Her grandmother is ill once more. She has been caring for two invalids."

"Will the grandmother be okay?"

"She is very old. It is unlikely that she will ever return home."

"Do you think she will die?"

"Yes, and very soon. I hope you will help Inga as she has helped you when that happens." I promised I would, but the effort of speaking had made me tired and I drifted off to sleep.

I awoke to the feel of a cool cloth washing my face.

"Good," Inga said. "You are going to get better."

"Yes. Thank you for everything."

"I only did what I needed to do. You have been asleep for a long time. Many people have asked after you. The most persistent of all is your friend Johnny. He comes by nearly every day. He is impatient for you to get well."

"I am tired," I said. "Very weak. Don't tell him I have improved for a few days." Then remembering the doctor, I asked after her grandmother.

"She is still alive," Inga said, "but she is not expected to live long."

"I'm sorry."

"Whatever must happen will happen. I have no power to change fate, so I must simply hope for the best." Inga left the room but came back in a few minutes with a cup of coffee. I drank it, and it was the first time I could remember enjoying food since I fell ill. Then she brought me a copy of *Njal's Saga* to read, and left me to myself. I soon fell into a confused sleep and when I awoke again it was dark. I walked out into the hallway and down the stairs to the dining room. Inga had left a plate of food and a glass of milk. I ate with real hunger, and felt stronger. And yet I didn't feel ready to meet anyone else. I didn't want to answer any questions. The world had moved on without me, and I wanted to feel my way back into it.

The next few days were among the happiest of my life. I slept for long hours, I walked around the house examining all the books and paintings and knick-knacks on the shelves. I looked at myself in the mirror and discovered that I had grown a beard. I read a couple of books, one of them a study of the tribes of Africa and the other a story of cowboys and Indians in the Wild West called *Deadwood Dick*. I walked over to Gudmundur Palsson's house and retrieved my guitar. There was only the housekeeper there, and she either did not know or did not want to tell me where the others were.

I practised for hours, and when Inga came in, I played for her. She wasn't around much, because she spent most of the time at her grandmother's bedside. The old lady was expected to die at any minute, but she seemed determined to hang on to life for as long as she could. Finally, after about a week, she did die. And the house was suddenly filled with people as Inga's family gathered for the funeral. I moved back to my room at Gudmundur Palsson's house, not sure I was still welcome, but the housekeeper seemed comfortable with my presence and she fed me.

Finally, I decided to pay a visit to Johnny to find out what had become of my money. He was at the café, drinking coffee and reading papers that he had spread out on the table.

"Baldur!" he shouted as I entered. "I had begun to think that you had gone to a better world than this one."

"No such luck," I told him. "I was just about to enter the Pearly Gates when I remembered that you still had my money, so I came back."

Johnny motioned me to silence and so I joined him at his table without saying anything. The waitress brought me a cup of coffee without my asking.

"You are lucky," Johnny said. "While you have been sleeping, your money has been working. With your information about the Icelanders' plans, I was able to get in early. They had to buy the lots we owned to put together their package. You now own five thousand dollars."

I could scarcely believe him. I had heard that money could multiply as if love were working in its body, but this was more money than I had ever imagined. I could buy a mansion with that much money. I could build a house in New Iceland for my parents and my brothers and sisters. I could keep my own team of horses.

"Unfortunately," he went on, "you won't see your money immediately. Another wonderful opportunity came along, and we are now partners in a warehouse in the business district. In less than a year we will double our money."

"That's great," I said, "but in the meanwhile I have no money, and I must pay for my keep. Inga has nursed me for nearly three months, and I must pay for my upkeep." My dreams of grandeur were beginning to vanish in the harsh light of the practical world.

"Don't worry about that," Johnny said. "I can keep you in spending money." He opened his wallet and handed me a small bundle of bills. "When you need more, just let me know. But remember that we are in a market that will pay every investment tenfold in the next few years. Try to save every dollar that you can to invest. And I want you to come to Toronto with me. There are people you must meet."

"When?"

"In a couple of weeks."

I had guessed that Lara's absence from her father's house probably meant that she was going to school in the east. This might be an opportunity to see her again. I agreed to accompany him. Then he showed me maps of Winnipeg on which he had written cryptic notes, and spoke of thousands of dollars until I could no longer follow him and my future seemed a matter of chance. He promised to get in touch with me in a short while, and I went back to Inga's grandmother's house. It seemed full of people, most of whom I had never seen before. Her father was there, and Flora had apparently accompanied Inga's brother Tomas. Everyone was grave, and the various conversations were conducted in whispers. The grandmother would be buried in two days at Brookside Cemetery. I was to come to the funeral. Would I sing at the service? Inga asked. I could not refuse, though I do not like funerals. Still, I had some experience in singing for the dead.

That night I returned to Gudmundur Palsson's house and found Gregory sitting in the music room. I asked him whether the others were expected home soon. He told me that Gudmundur was in New York on business, and that Lara was now attending school in Toronto and would not be back until Easter.

"I hear you have been busy," Gregory said.

"Yes," I answered, "but I have been ill for a long time. I am only now recovered."

"So I have heard. But you still found time to make some excellent investments."

"I had some advice from a friend."

"Well, your friend may be playing out a game he doesn't understand. I'd be careful of his advice if I were you. And I hope you are not telling him things you have heard here. Gudmundur Palsson would be unhappy if you did that." Gudmundur Palsson's happiness was not my main priority, but I did not say that. Instead, I asked for the name of the school that Lara attended.

"She is attending the Bishop Strachan School, a very exclusive school for girls." I wanted to ask for more details, but I did not want to rouse any suspicions that I might try to see Lara there, and so I went on to ask about Gudmundur Palsson and his business in New York.

"Gudmundur is interested in railways," Gregory told me. "And railways are an important development in this country and particularly in this province." After that we chattered about the weather and Gregory left me saying he was going to do the books. I took my guitar and practised for a few moments, but my mind was not in it. I thought that I would have to meet with Johnny and plan our trip to Toronto.

The funeral took place on a bright, warm March day. Snow was melting, and the streets were full of mud. I sang "O Gud vors lands" because Inga said it was her grandmother's favourite song. After the church service, we went out to the cemetery west of the city where Inga's grandmother was laid to rest. The minister conducted the service entirely in English, and when it was over we returned to the house for a reception. People milled about eating dainties and drinking coffee. Inga drew me aside and said, "My grandmother has left this house to me."

"It is a wonderful house," I told her. "You are very fortunate."

"I cannot stay here," she said. "I have no money and no job. I will have to sell it."

"Did your grandmother leave no money?"

"Yes, but she left it to other people, my father and my brother and several cousins."

"You could take in boarders to help pay expenses."

"Where will I find these wealthy boarders who will pay me enough money?"

"You could find me, for instance."

"You? You have no money, and you are unlikely to make much playing a guitar."

"I have money," I told her. "I have made some good investments and I can afford to pay for my keep."

"How did you make these investments lying on your back in bed?" she asked. "I know that you had no money when you became ill." I told her then about Johnny, about the investment we had made and my five thousand dollars. I told her that I expected to make a good deal more in the future, and I would help her to keep the house. She seemed doubtful.

"I don't know whether my father would permit it," she said. "But I will consult with him and let you know his decision in a couple of days. I must have somewhere to stay if I am to remain in Winnipeg and study, so I may be able to convince him. I had to leave the normal school to nurse the two of you, but they say that they will take me back."

The next day, I didn't have much to do, so I wandered down to the restaurant I had begun to think of as Johnny's restaurant. He wasn't at his usual table, but the waitress told me he was probably at his warehouse on Princess Street. She didn't know the number, but said it was just a few doors down from McDermot.

I walked over to Princess and found the corner with McDermot. There were a number of warehouses in the area, and the people at the first one I tried had never heard of Johnny. The second one had his name painted on the door, so I went in. Johnny was sitting in a small office with glass windows. He waved me to come in and I did.

"This," he said, "is our warehouse. Would you like to have your name painted on the door?" I told him I thought not. I didn't think many people would come looking for me, and it would simply be misleading.

"Suit yourself. But I have already had an offer for the place. I think if we hang on for another couple of months we can get double the amount that we paid for it."

"Great," I said. "And what about our trip to Toronto?"

"Soon enough, my man. I am waiting for a letter that should come some time in the next ten days. Can you be ready to leave on short notice?"

"I can go this minute if you want."

"No, we'll wait for the letter. I've contacted a number of investors who I hope will put up the money for a couple of other projects that I'll tell you about on the train to Toronto."

The thought of the train trip excited me. I had never travelled before, but since my shoeshining days I had wanted to go somewhere by train.

Johnny showed me around the warehouse. It was an enormous place, three stories tall with an elevator and with dozens of people working. They carried boxes that gave no indication of their content, but everybody seemed terribly busy. I asked Johnny what was in the boxes.

"Mostly farm implements, plows and harnesses and axes and hammers and parts of wagons and sleighs. Stuff like that. The boxes come in from the east, and are distributed throughout the west from here."

When I went back to Inga's that night, most of the family had gone back to New Iceland. Her father was reluctant to allow her to keep the house. He thought that she should sell it and take room and board. She had argued that it could save the family a lot of money since they would now have a house to stay in when they came to the city and so they would not have to pay for hotels. He said he would make his decision in a couple of days.

"It's your house," I told Inga.

"Not really. My father has control of my finances and I must do what he says."

"Tell him of my offer," I said.

"I have."

"Then let's hope for the best." I made my way back to my room at Gudmundur Palsson's house, and read from *Njal's Saga* until I fell asleep.

For the next couple of days I was at loose ends. I took the streetcar down Main Street to the very end and rode back. Many of the people riding in the car were Ukrainians. The women wore colourful headscarves and the men were in sheepskin coats, though the weather had warmed up considerably. The children were silent, but their parents spoke loudly in a language I had never heard before. We passed the new city hall, resplendent in its bright pink glory. The Slavs pointed out the building to their children, and everyone seemed excited to see it.

I got off at Rupert Avenue and walked back on the west side of Main Street. There were a lot of Indians in the city that day, dressed in skins decorated with beads. They carried trunks with them, and I wondered what those trunks contained. The group that was walking just in front of me turned off at Market Street and I followed them for a while. They went into a warehouse just down the street from the one that I apparently owned with Johnny. Since I was so near, I dropped in at our warehouse. Johnny was exactly where I had last left him, sitting in his chair at a desk on the other side of the glass window.

"Any news?" I asked.

"Yes there is," he said. "We leave for Toronto in two days. We'll be gone a week, including travelling both ways." He reached into a drawer and passed me an envelope. "Here's your ticket, a few dollars to spend and a map of Toronto in case you get lost."

"When do we leave?"

"Sunday at noon. Meet me at the station."

"Good. I'll see you then," I said and took my leave. I checked out how much money I had been given. There was a good deal more than I expected to need, so I stopped off at a clothing store on Portage Avenue and bought myself a suit. I had never expected to need a suit, but now that my fortunes had changed I thought I should try to live up to my success. In another store just a few doors away, I saw a beautiful leather bag in the window. The clerk informed me that it was a Gladstone bag, and I bought it and carried it home. The next day I packed the bag and waited for the day to pass so I could leave for the east.

The next day I stopped off at Inga's house to tell her I would be gone for a week to Toronto on business. She was in high spirits. Her father had agreed that I might board there for a year, and then we would review the arrangement. He had decided that the rent should be five dollars a week. I agreed and gave Inga the first month's rent. She wanted me to choose my room, but I said there would be plenty of time when I returned.

The train wound through a few miles of flat prairie before bursting into a landscape I had never imagined. The land became increasingly hilly and thickly forested with spruce and pine. Every few miles we passed a lake and from the window of the train we could see moose and black bears and wolves. There were few human settlements, and those we saw were isolated shanties that looked as if those who lived in them had given up trying to improve their lot. The train stopped from time to time for no understandable reason. But the rhythm of the wheels clanking on the rails was hypnotic, and I soon fell asleep.

I awoke when Johnny shook me awake and told me it was time to eat. The dining car was elegantly furnished, with white table-cloths and fancy silverware. We dined on trout and drank wine from a pitcher the waiter brought us. It was a more lavish meal than I had ever had in a restaurant. After we had eaten, Johnny offered me a cigar. I had never smoked one before, but I thought I should try. Johnny cautioned me not to inhale, and after one small coughing fit I learned how to hold in the smoke and release it without filling my lungs. And yet it didn't taste very good, and I wasn't sure why people smoked. Johnny said that after a few more cigars, I would learn to appreciate the taste.

"We are going to meet with a few capitalists who want to invest in the Great Northwest, as they call it. They know there are fortunes to be made, but it is difficult to learn in Toronto what is going to happen in Winnipeg. Our advantage is that we are on the spot and we know where the next important development is going to take place. Or at least we have to convince them that we know, so they will invest in us." He brought some papers out of his leather case and told me I would have to sign them. The papers referred to a company called The Manitoba Development Trust. "That company is us," Johnny said. "You are the president, and I am the secretary-treasurer."

"Why am I president?" I asked.

"You are president because you have a clear record. A few years ago I tried to invest without enough capital, and there was some nasty business with the police. That's all behind us now, but it is still better that you present the face of the company." I filled out the form and gave Inga's house as my address.

"Excellent," Johnny said. "That is a fine address for a rich man. And they will notice that."

"But I don't really understand what we are doing, so I am sure to make blunders that will give us away. We are not actually financiers or real estate men or whatever. At least I am not, and I don't think I can pretend to be."

"All you have to do is shake hands, say a few words about the weather, and introduce me as your assistant. I will make the presentation. They will not make a decision while we are there. We will go back to the hotel and wait for them to call."

I agreed that I would try, though I was not confident. By now night had fallen and the train was a travelling light in the darkness. There was nothing to see from the windows as we made our way to the Pullman car to sleep. I was sure that I would lie awake all night, but I had hardly begun to dream before light poured in and we were in another landscape. Here the land had been cleared and there were farms and well-developed towns. We could see people everywhere, riding in carriages, walking, or even on bicycles.

When the train stopped we stepped out into a railway station that made the Winnipeg station look like a small-town stop. The roof was high, and pigeons flew everywhere. Dozens of trains waited on many tracks. People were lined up everywhere, and they pushed and shoved each other. Vendors cried out their wares, as the crowd swept by them like a relentless river.

Outside, the city was loud and frantic. Everyone seemed in a terrible rush, and we had to move smartly to avoid being run over. People were walking dogs on leashes, and a cat slept on the balcony of almost every business we passed. We walked down Queen Street past Yonge to our hotel.

Our first meeting was the following day. Johnny had not slept well on the train so he wanted to rest. I told him that I would go out for a walk, but would meet him for supper. I took my map and left the room. The clerk was behind his desk in the lobby reading a newspaper. I asked him if he could give me directions to the Bishop Strachan School. He said he wasn't sure but thought it might be on College Street.

"There's a place that used to be called Wykeham Hall that was converted into a girl's school. It's not far from here." He took my map and searched it for a while. Then he marked an X on the map and said, "I think that's the place. You can find out soon enough if you take a walk there."

I walked out into the bustling street. The map was helpful, but it was not as easy to find my directions as the clerk had suggested. After about an hour of walking and asking directions of passers-by, I found myself hopelessly lost. Then, just as I was about to ask another store-keeper for directions back to my hotel, I saw a brick building with the name Wykeham Hall on it. I walked past it and then returned. I suddenly felt overwhelmed. I had found the place but I was no nearer to finding Lara than if I had stayed in Winnipeg. I could not just walk into the school and look for her. And I could think of no way that I could explain to the authorities of the school that I had a good reason for meeting her.

I stood across from the school for about fifteen minutes waiting to see if she might come out. After a while several girls did come out. They were all wearing uniforms, and any one of them might have been Lara. I gave up waiting and returned to the hotel, but I made sure I could find my way back to the school.

Johnny was in a good mood when I returned. He was rested and eager for us to begin our business. We had supper in the hotel res-taurant and Johnny ordered a bottle of wine. "We have two meet-ings tomorrow," he said, "and these are the most important of our contacts. If we can get the support of at least one of these groups, then our fortunes are made." I wanted to go to bed early, but Johnny wanted to go out to a little bar he knew. The bar was only a few minutes' walk away and inside it was bright and inviting. A beauti-ful young woman dressed in what appeared to be a man's suit was singing. The patrons were all smoking cigars, and it was hard to see through the blue smoke. I ordered a beer and Johnny had a glass of rye whisky. We joined the others in smoking cigars, and I guess I must have inhaled more than I thought because by the time we left I was feeling ill.

I was worried that I would be too sick in the morning to attend the meetings, but I awoke clear-headed and full of enthusiasm. We had breakfast at the hotel and headed out for our first meeting. To my surprise, the meeting was in a boardroom in the hotel itself. Three heavy-set men in three-piece blue suits were waiting for us when we arrived. They looked like men who ate well, and the suits seemed almost a uniform.

I introduced myself and shook hands with each of them. Then I introduced Johnny as my assistant and told the men he would make our presentation. Johnny may have been nervous, but he didn't show it. He drew a series of papers and maps from his leather case and spread them out on the table. Soon he was extolling the virtues of Winnipeg and talking about the profits to be made there. He said he expected another one hundred thousand people to arrive over the next ten years. All these people would need to be housed. And there were carpenters and plumbers and painters and masons who would come to build these houses, and they would also have to be housed. He talked not of individual houses but of blocks of houses. He talked about the difficulty of getting permits without knowing the people who controlled the permits, and he implied that we knew what palms would have to be greased to make our schemes work.

Then he described an area where he said would be the next big development. He did not, however, tell where this area was or when the land would be coming up for sale. He said that once we had made a partnership agreement, then he would provide the other details. After about an hour, the men withdrew to consider our offer. A few moments later another contingent arrived, four men this time in the same blue three-piece suits as the others. Johnny made the same pitch to these men and I was amazed that he could say the same thing almost verbatim that he had told the others.

"They are tough groups, both of them," he told me. "They have money but they don't like to part with it. I've let them know that this is about risk, but that the risk in Winnipeg is much less than leaving their money in a bank in Toronto." I had no way of knowing whether to be optimistic or pessimistic about our prospects, but Johnny said a guarded optimism was the best policy.

On the way back to the hotel I told Johnny that I wanted to go for a walk to clear my head, but I would meet him back at the hotel for supper. Then I made my way to the Bishop Strachan School. This time I had more luck. Three young women came down the street toward me, and one of them was Lara. I called out her name and she hurried over to me. She didn't seem the least surprised to see me.

"Meet me tomorrow at the little café just around the corner. It's called the Blue Café. Come at exactly the same time as now. I have to run because I don't want anyone to get suspicious." And she rejoined the other girls, and they all walked to the café and entered. I went back to the hotel, still uncertain what I would say to her when we met.

The following day we had one meeting in the morning. This time there was only one man, a slim young fellow in a long overcoat. He wore a rose in his lapel that gave him the air of a dandy. He was whistling to himself when we arrived, and he was the most remarkable whistler. I did not recognize the tune he was whistling, but I recognized the craft, and I commented on it. He was pleased at the compliment but demurred that it was nothing, just something his father had taught him. He introduced himself as Robert Hawkins and Johnny gave him the same spiel that he had given the other men. Hawkins barely glanced at the documents.

"Yes, yes, I know," he said. "There are fortunes to be made. And I know you are looking for capital. I cannot provide the capital that some others can, but I can pull my weight, and I know how to raise capital here. In my law practice I meet a lot of rich men who would like to invest, but to be frank, gentlemen, they would probably not trust you. I am looking for a partnership with men like yourselves who have ideas and inside knowledge. Are you interested in forming a partnership?"

I liked Robert Hawkins, but I knew so little about business that I had no idea what to say. Johnny said he would have to hear the details of the proposed partnership before he could make any commitment. Hawkins invited us to lunch and then to a visit at his office where he would explain the details. I agreed to join them for lunch but said I would leave Johnny to sort out details. I hinted that I had an important previous engagement; Johnny frowned, and I knew he didn't believe me, but I thought I could explain later.

Over lunch, Hawkins told stories about men who had become rich and men who had lost their shirts. "Everybody suffers from Manitoba Fever right now," he said. "Men come back with tales of making fortunes, but they also come back saddened and chastened. I had thought of moving to Manitoba myself, but I think that a partnership where Toronto money and Manitoba knowledge worked together would be the best option."

Johnny nodded agreement. He seemed to be warming up to Hawkins, though he seemed far from actually agreeing to anything. The waitress brought the bill and Hawkins seized it, insisting we were his guests. Johnny provided a tip so large I thought the waitress might quit her job right then, but she didn't blink an eye and pocketed the money with a polite, "Thank you, sir."

I took my leave and headed out to the Bishop Strachan School. The weather was excellent. The sun shone and sparrows sang in the trees. An old dog adopted me and followed me along the street. I stopped to pet it, and it rolled on its back with delight. I reached the school about a half-hour early with the dog in tow. There was nothing to see at the school, so I walked down College Street, looking in the windows.

When I finally made my way to the café, Lara was already there, drinking a cup of coffee. She was still in her uniform, which made her look much younger than she was.

"Hello," I said.

"Hello, yourself," she answered. "What are you doing in this part of the world?"

"I'm here on business," I said. "I'm here with Johnny. We're trying to find financing for a couple of business ventures."

"So you've become a businessman. A man of high finance who travels to other cities to find money."

I didn't like the way the conversation was going so I asked her how life at the school was.

"A minor hell on earth," she told me. "A million ridiculous rules, hours of studying ancient history and dead languages, mathematics that I will never use in a lifetime, and rules of etiquette and decorum. In case I become the wife of the prime minister. Which I will never do."

"Not much fun?"

"Not much fun at all. But tonight we will have fun. I've checked out of the school until tomorrow night. My elderly aunt is ill, and I have to go and visit her."

"I'm sorry to hear that."

"No, you're not. You are my elderly aunt, and we're going to spend a night to remember. Now you wait here while I go to the bathroom to change." She picked up a small bag from the floor beside her chair and vanished down a flight of steps. In a short time she was back, dressed in a skirt and jacket that entirely removed her schoolgirl look.

"You look great," I told her.

"Do you have any money?"

I assured her that I had all the money we would need.

"Good," she said, "because I have some serious partying to do before I am once more incarcerated. Let's go."

We walked out into the streets that were now becoming active. People were rushing in all directions. A man came by carrying a bouquet of red roses, and a gang of children ran down the street shouting in some language I did not recognize. We walked for about a quarter of an hour, and I had no idea where we were going. Finally, Lara said, "This is it," and she led me into the fanciest restaurant I had ever seen. The tables were covered with white linen and each table had a candle on it.

"Give me ten dollars," she said, and I gave it to her. When the waiter arrived with our menus, she passed him the money and whispered something to him. "I think this will work," she said.

The waiter was back almost immediately with a bottle of clear liquid and a couple of bottles of orange juice. He wished to take our order, but Lara said that she would order after a while. Then she poured some of the clear liquid into each of our glasses and filled them up with orange juice. We clicked our glasses and drank. I was surprised by the power of the liquid and nearly choked on my first mouthful.

"Gin," Lara said. "Do you like it?"

I tasted another mouthful and found it quite agreeable. "It's fine," I said. "But women are not supposed to drink in public places. How did you get the liquor?"

"You bribed the waiter."

"How did you know he would accept a bribe?"

"Lydia and Barbara told me about this place. They're classmates. They each have boyfriends, and they come here whenever they can. I, unfortunately, do not have a boyfriend in Toronto, so while they carouse, I study Greek history. You have no idea how happy I was to see you yesterday."

"What if I had no money?"

"I have money of my own." She took another mouthful from her glass and gave a little shudder. "I had got used to having a nip of gin most days when I was at home in Winnipeg. My father keeps a well-stocked bar, and he never notices whether anything is gone. The school is as dry as the Sahara." She downed the rest of her drink and poured herself another.

"We should be careful how much we drink," I told her.

"You be careful how much you drink," she answered. "I am going to have some fun."

The waiter returned and we ordered from the menu. I had a rack of lamb, and Lara ordered *foie gras* and trout. Lara was a little drunk already, and she chattered on about the school and the girls there. Many of them had apparently been sent there because of their behaviour, and Lara seemed to approve strongly of the behaviour that had brought them there. After the meal was over, Lara asked another ten dollars and she gave it to the waiter. He returned with a brown paper bag she put into the bag with her clothes. We walked down the streets of Toronto under the gas lamps, and Lara insisted that I sing for her. I did, and the people we passed all seemed surprised and delighted to hear me singing.

Soon it was getting late, and I knew I would have to get Lara to wherever she was staying while she was still reasonably sober. "Where are you going to stay?" I asked her.

"What do you mean?"

"Where are you going to sleep tonight?"

"Tell me where you are going to sleep." I told her I would sleep at my hotel.

"Then that's where I'll sleep," she said.

"Have you no place to go?"

"No, only the school. And if I come in late and drunk they will expel me, and my father will be angry." We were near the hotel, so I invited her up to my room. We crossed the wide waiting room, walked past the deep leather chairs and made our way up the broad stone stairs. I opened the door with the big brass key that the door-man had given me on my arrival. The room had heavy crimson curtains, a couple of armchairs and a large bed with a feather quilt. Lara did a little dance, then pulled back the curtains and looked out onto the street. She took the bottle of gin out of the brown paper bag and poured us each another drink. We drank in silence for a few moments.

"You can sleep in the bed," I told her. "I will sleep on the floor."

"I have to pee," she said, and went into the bathroom. I looked out the window at the lights of Toronto and wondered what Gudmundur Palsson would do if he discovered that his daughter had spent the night with me. I didn't know what he could do, but I was pretty sure I did not want to find out.

The bathroom door opened, and Lara walked into the room completely naked. She was even more beautiful than when she was dressed. She moved into my arms and gave me a long passionate kiss that ended all hope of my behaving rationally. I took off my clothes and got into bed with her. Her skin was amazingly smooth and cool.

"I've never done this before," I told her.

"Neither have I," she said. "But there has to be a first time, and I always knew it would be you." Then we kissed again and we managed our lovemaking without any instruction. It was much easier then I had imagined. Lara fell asleep as soon as it was over, but I lay awake for hours wondering about what would happen to me in this world. And marvelling at what had already happened.

When I awoke the next day, Lara was gone. She had not left a note or any trace that she had been here with me at the hotel. I felt a sickening sense of loss, but at the same time a strange relief. I did not want to encounter her with a hangover or have to take her back to the school. I felt that the event would be best in memory rather than as a sudden complication in my life. I could not stay in Toronto, and I hoped both that I would see her soon and that I would not.

I met Johnny for breakfast. He was just finishing his coffee when I arrived in the restaurant of the hotel. I ordered coffee and toast, and asked about his meeting with Hawkins. He told me that he and Hawkins had made an agreement. We were to outline a project, and he would find venture money for it. We would split any profits that we made. None of the others we had met with had returned any answer to our proposals.

"That's their problem," he told me. "Let them invest in Toronto, and see how much that makes them." We had one more meeting, he told me, with a man named Parkinson. I finished my breakfast and we went up to the boardroom and found an extremely fat man in a suit that fit him badly. Johnny delivered his proposal, which by now he could do so smoothly it seemed like a memorized theatre piece. After it was over, Parkinson said he thought he could work with us. He told us to provide all the details of our next project, and he would finance it. I didn't think we could trust him, but Johnny said that in matters of finance, appearances meant nothing. Only actual cash counted.

That afternoon I walked over to the school and went to the café where I had met Lara. I thought she might appear, but she did not. Several girls from the school came in laughing, but they did not acknowledge me in any way. I went back to the hotel where Johnny was already packing for the next day's return to Winnipeg.

The train trip was uneventful. We passed the same hills and lakes and trees we had passed on our way east, and the landscape was as empty of human presence as it had been before. When we pulled into the CPR station in Winnipeg, I felt a huge sense of release. Johnny and I agreed to meet in one week's time, and I made my way to Inga's place. She had given me a key, so I did not bother to knock. There was no one at home, but she had left a note saying that her mother was ill, and she had gone back to New Iceland to take care of her. I decided at that moment that I would make a visit to New Iceland myself. I had not seen my parents or my brothers and sisters for several months. It was time to go back.

I wanted to go back as a success rather than as a lost and failed son returning to the fold, so I spent the next three days buying presents for the family. I wasn't sure what they would like, but I trusted the clerks at the stores to advise me, and when I took the coach down to Gimli, I had so many presents there was not much room for other passengers. Not that there were many other passengers. My sole companion was the older Icelandic woman who had attended my concert at Gudmundur Palsson's. She was pleased to see me, and chatted on without encouragement. She invited me to come to church in Winnipeg and sing for the congregation. I refused as politely as I could, explaining that I had suffered a cold that had somehow damaged my vocal cords, and I would not be able to sing for several months. That was not entirely a lie since I had found it difficult to sing after my illness.

I had sent word that I was coming, and the whole family was there to meet me when I arrived. Apparently my good luck and improved position in the world had not escaped their notice. I warned them not to open any of the packages until we were home, and they agreed, though the younger ones seemed quite disappointed. My mother had made an elaborate supper for us all, and when it was over I allowed the children to tear open the packages. Apparently the store clerks who advised me had not been mistaken. There were squeals of delight and a couple of trades made, and they were finally sent off to bed. My father, my mother, the brother and Flora and my sister all stayed up. My father offered me a glass of whisky, and the brother found his own glass. I presented each of them with a cigar, and we lit up and drank to good fortune.

I had bought dresses and scarves for my mother and the girls and they were happy with my choices. The brother got a rifle, the younger boys pocket knives, and my father a wallet with a hundred dollars in it. It turned out both my father and the brother were more familiar with the effects of whisky, and I went to bed leaving them smoking and singing.

The next morning I was up bright and early. There was still no bed for me so I slept on the couch in the living room. By the time the room was bright, a pair of tiny girls had climbed on top of me and were holding my eyelids open to see whether I was inside. My mother had already made coffee and oatmeal porridge, so I breakfasted while my father and the brother slept on.

I excused myself and walked out to my favourite place in New Iceland, the graveyard where the sleepers on the roofs had gone to their long rest. I bid them good morning, apologized for my long absence and whistled the "Ode to Joy" for them. They gave no reply, but I was sure it was only that they were unused to speech, having rested so long under the earth. After a while, I heard a sound like distant voices or the sighing of leaves in the trees in a gentle breeze.

Then, just as I thought they might have a message for me, I caught sight of a figure slipping through the trees at the edge of the graveyard. At first I thought it was Lara, but when I walked to the edge of the bush I saw that it was Flora, in the bright blue dress I had bought for her. She was weeping quietly, so I asked what was wrong.

"Everything," she said. "Everything is wrong."

"Tell me more."

"Tomas wishes to marry me. He asks me every day. I love him very much, but I cannot marry him. You know what I have been. If he ever found out he would never forgive me, and he would be unhappy for the rest of his life." I knew of course that she was right. But perhaps I have an insufficient moral character. I didn't see that some rigid honesty was a better choice than a lie that would allow two people in love to live together.

"Where did you grow up?" I asked her.

"In Picton, Ontario. I moved to Winnipeg with my mother and father when I was fourteen. Shortly after we arrived here, my parents both died and I was left alone. Minnie took me in or I should have starved to death."

"Does anyone in Picton know what has become of you?"

"No, I have had no contact with anyone there since I left."

"Then there is no problem," I told her. "You shall marry Tomas and move back to Picton."

"But how could we live? Tomas is a fisherman. He doesn't have any other trade."

"I will see to it that he has a boat and nets and enough money for the two of you to get started. Picton, you will remember, is on a lake."

"Where will this money come from?"

"Business. I am now in the real estate business, and I have quite a lot of money and expect more soon. But I will have to swear you to secrecy. The offer to Tomas will come from a mysterious company in Toronto. Under no circumstances let him know that I am involved."

Flora agreed, and she left a much happier girl than she had been an hour earlier. I turned back to the sleepers in the graveyard, but they refused to speak to me. I whistled tunes for them once more, some short Icelandic lullabies, but even that did not console them.

When I got back, the brother was dressed in oilskins, preparing to go out and lift his nets. He asked if I wanted to go with him and I agreed. I had watched the fishermen going out to fish and returning with their catch when I was younger, but I had never gone out on the lake myself. The brother told me as we loaded nets into the boat that he was worried about my father.

"He is too friendly with the whisky bottle," Geiri said. "He drinks nearly every day."

"I noticed last night that you were pretty friendly with it yourself."

"Yes," he said, "but I drink only on a special occasion. Our father drinks too much."

There was a gentle swell to the lake, but the sun was bright and the seagulls and pelicans followed us as we left the dock and sailed out into the lake. The brother handled the ropes of the rigging of our two-masted sailing skiff. His nets were set about a mile from shore, marked by blue-flagged buoys. We worked intently, untangling the fish from the seine and flipping them into wooden boxes. The brother was much faster than I was, and it sometimes seemed that I was not helping him, but merely getting in the way.

"I'll fillet when we get back," I told him. "I have no experience on the lake, but I can fillet a fish with the best of them." We tossed the junk fish out of the boat, and the pelicans and gulls fought for them. One pelican actually landed on the prow of the boat, and the brother tossed it small fish that it caught and swallowed.

When we were finished and heading back to shore, the brother brought out up the topic of our father once more. "He's hopeless," he said. "He's found two young boys, some sort of cousins, he says, and he's brought them home to live with us."

"Maybe I could help. I've come into some money and I could get the family a bigger house."

"What would be the point? He'd only fill it with more lost souls, and our mother would have to feed them. I tell you, the man is crazed."

Back on shore, we filleted the fish, and I was glad to notice that I was both faster and cleaner at filleting than the brother. I swore him to secrecy and told him that Flora would be marrying soon, and moving to Ontario. That would give them all a bit more room.

"Is that the truth now?" he said. "I thought she had some deep dark secret that would prevent the wedding. She's sure led the fellow a merry chase."

"Not so deep and not so dark. They'll be going to Picton in Ontario, where she was born and where he can fish. But you can go and visit them."

"No, I don't think so. If I can travel it will be to Vancouver, where the weather is warmer and the fishing is better. Can I tell you a secret?"

"Yes."

"I'll be going in the fall. And I don't think I'll ever come back here."

"Have you fallen in love, and is that the reason?"

"Yes and no. I've fallen in love but the object of my desire has not so far declared her love for me. But her parents are moving to Vancouver, and she is going with them. And so I go west to press my suit."

There wasn't much to say after that. We went back to the house where the children were playing some game that required that they scream at the tops of their voices. The brother quieted the house by sending them all into the yard to play except the baby and Joa, who now started to weep at the departure of the others. Fortunately, our mother rocked them each for a few minutes and they fell asleep.

After supper, the brother excused himself and walked down the road to the village. Our father waited till he was out of earshot, then he asked me, "Have you noticed anything strange about your brother?"

I told him no, that I hadn't, and he went on to explain. "Your brother has become depressed and morose. He mopes around the place and has no desire to do anything. He complains incessantly about the noise and takes long walks by himself."

"Sounds like love to me," I said.

"Now, you might have something there," our father said. "I hadn't thought about that. Love. Who would have expected such a development? And who do you think he might have fallen in love with?"

I told him that I hadn't any idea, but the world was full of people falling in love with each other every day. There was nothing unusual about the brother's case.

"And you?" our father asked. "Are you also in love?" I told him that I was always in love, that I had been in love as long as I could remember. He didn't press me further to ask for specific names. I gave him a cigar, and he poured me a glass of whisky and we went out onto the porch and smoked until the moon was high in the sky.

I asked him about his plan to take a dog team to the States, and I apologized for not having responded.

"You were sick," he said. "I didn't expect a response. It had to do with exploring in the Arctic. They offered excellent money, but I decided it was too dangerous." He took a deep drag on his cigar, and asked what I was doing now. I told him about Johnny and our real estate deals.

"Well, did you discover anything in Toronto that will make you a rich man?" I told him that I had noticed in Toronto that there were many apartment blocks where dozens of families lived in a single building. People in Winnipeg were in desperate need of housing, and

I thought that whoever started to build apartment blocks there would soon be rich. I had not thought of this while I was in Toronto, but our father's question had made me think.

"I guess you better go back to Winnipeg and build some," he said. I wasn't sure whether he was serious or sarcastic, but I did intend to get back as soon as possible and talk to Johnny about my idea.

The next morning I went to say goodbye to the dead in the cemetery. I saw a man and a woman talking intently at the far side, near the edge of the bush. I recognized the brother, and the woman with him was Elin, the girl I had taught English to in what seemed like another lifetime. They kissed, and I moved on past the small clump of trees near the gate so that I would not seem to be spying on them. They both came to the gate, but they parted there and went in different directions. I saw, though, that just as they were parting, Elin gave the brother a white lace handkerchief that he put in his pocket. After they were gone, I spoke to the dead, but they were unresponsive. I looked for movement in the trees, half-believing that Lara might appear, but there was nothing but the twitter of a wren and the cry of seagulls from the lake.

I waited until mid-afternoon to go see Inga and find out how her mother was feeling, though that had been one of the main reasons for my return to New Iceland. Her father greeted me at the door and welcomed me in. Tomas and Flora were sitting together in the kitchen drinking coffee. They greeted me warmly and invited me to join them. The four of us sat there at the table in an awkward silence, until finally Flora said, "Inga will be back in a minute. She has gone to get the homeopath. The doctor can do nothing, but Inga thinks that Mrs. Hjalmarson may be able to help."

I knew Halla Hjalmarson. She had been to our house several times when the children were sick, and they had always improved after her visit. If anyone could help, it would be her.

"I don't believe in that kind of medicine," Inga's father said. "That kind of healing is pure superstition. If the doctor cannot help, then there is no help to be had."

"But your wife believes in Mrs. Hjalmarson, and sometimes believing is better than medicine," Flora told him.

"We will see."

A few minutes later Inga arrived, accompanied by a wide and cheerful woman in a green dress. Mrs. Hjalmarson wore a bright red scarf, and several necklaces. She had so many bracelets that she jangled as she walked. She paid no attention to our sombre group at the kitchen table, but followed Inga into the bedroom where her mother lay. We could hear Mrs. Hjalmarson's cheerful voice as she talked to Inga's mother. She asked dozens of questions that seemed to have nothing to do with illness. Finally, she came out into the kitchen and told us, "The doctor could not cure her because there is nothing wrong with her. She is simply depressed. She has no small children any more, and because she is the mayor's wife, she has no work to do. She must go back to the city with Inga and live with her for six months. She must go out to as many concerts and meetings as she can. By the end of six months, she will be fine, but the mayor may have to find more things for her to do, or she will fall into the same malaise again."

After she had left, Inga's mother walked into the room and sat down at the table. She asked for a cup of coffee. Tomas and his father were amazed. "You haven't been out of bed for a month," Tomas said.

"I had no reason to get out of bed. But I am up now, and I must get packed if I am to go to the city with Inga tomorrow."

The mayor seemed distressed. "But how am I to get by?" he asked. "Who will cook the food and clean the house?"

"Just pretend that I am dead," she answered. "And then you will find some way."

Inga's mother certainly didn't look sick to me. And she bustled about getting ready, choosing the clothes she would take and the jewellery she would wear. Inga asked me to accompany her to Thorkellsson's store to buy some food so that Tomas and her father would not starve until they figured out how to fend for themselves.

As soon as we were out in the street, Inga said, "I knew immediately that there was nothing wrong with my mother except boredom.

My father is proud of how he runs a disciplined household just as he runs a well-organized town. But my mother has always wanted to live in the city, and she had decided that she would either get her desire or lie in her bed until she died."

"So we will all go back to the city tomorrow?"

"Yes. And thank you for your help with Tomas and Flora."

"Flora told you?"

"Yes."

"But she was sworn to secrecy."

"You don't know much about women, do you? Flora would have exploded if she hadn't told someone. But don't worry. Your secret is safe with me."

The next morning, I bade goodbye to my family, including the two new cousins who had arrived from Riverton to live with us, and I walked over to Inga's and helped her carry her mother's bags to the coach. The trip to Winnipeg was uneventful, except that Inga's mother spoke incessantly about her plans. I was amazed at how much she knew about the concerts she intended to attend and the organizations she would join. She pointed out houses and animals as we passed, and she seemed almost manic in her happiness.

We stopped briefly in Selkirk to change horse teams and drivers. Inga went into the stable to look around and returned with a small puppy. It was low to the ground with wiry hair and a sort of scrubby beard. It ran with a bouncing motion so that its ears flapped, and it barked a tiny, joyous bark.

"His name is Dalgleish," she said. "He's some sort of Scottish dog. The driver's dog had six puppies, and if I hadn't taken him he would have been killed."

"A dog is a lot of work," I said. "And they poop in your yard and you have to clean it up."

"That's not your problem," Inga told me. "I am already hopelessly in love with this dog." She wrapped it up in the blanket that she had spread across her lap, so that only its head stuck out. It looked triumphant, as if it knew of its astonishing good luck. I reached out to pet it, and it bit me a little sharp bite, but it didn't growl or bark. I could see that as long as I lived in Inga's house, I was going to have to strike up a relationship with this creature.

When we arrived at the house, Inga's mother went from room to room to choose where she would stay. The room she chose was the one I had already chosen. Inga began to tell her mother that she could not stay there, but I intervened and said I would be perfectly happy in another room. The puppy was as excited as Inga's mother, and it ran through the entire house, smelling every bit of furniture and leaping up on chairs and sofas. Inga spoke sternly to the creature, but it paid her no heed. Finally, I let it out the back door into the fenced-in backyard, where it burned up more energy investigating every tree and shrub and chasing a red squirrel. After about a half-hour it scratched at the door. I let it in, and it found a spot on the rug and immediately fell asleep.

The next day I went down to the warehouse to see Johnny. He was as usual shuffling papers when I arrived. He asked where I had been, and I told him about my trip to New Iceland.

"I've just received news from Hawkins in Toronto," Johnny said. "He has lined up a batch of investors. Now all we have to do is provide a project that excites them and we're underway."

"I have the project," I told Johnny. "We are going to build apartment blocks. You saw the huge blocks filled with families in Toronto. But there are none in Winnipeg. If the city is going to grow as fast as you say, then the people who come are going to need some place to stay. There aren't enough houses, and anyway the houses in Winnipeg are too expensive for working people. What do you think?"

Johnny stared at me without blinking for a long minute. Then he leaped from his chair and clapped me on the back. "Brilliant," he said. "An absolutely brilliant idea. I should have thought of it myself." He began to shuffle his papers again. "We have an offer for the warehouse. I was going to turn it down and wait, but this is too important."

"Why are we going to sell the warehouse?"

"Because we have to invest in the apartment blocks ourselves. We will not be mere traders investing other people's money. We will be capitalists ourselves, partners with Hawkins, and we will make a great deal of money." He shoved a sheaf of papers over to me and told me to sign. "That's the bill of sale for the warehouse. Now we have to look for an office and we need a name. And we need to hire some good workers as soon as possible."

I thought of the Icelanders who were working for the railway. "I can hire Icelanders for you. Preferably some who don't speak too much English. They'll stick together and they'll be loyal."

"Do they know how to build?" Johnny asked.

"Yes," I told him, though I had very little idea what kind of workers they were. But I knew how hard the fishermen worked, and I thought if they worked as hard at building as they did at fishing, we would do well.

"Good, then," Johnny said. You go and find about twenty workers, and I'll get back to Hawkins about the money."

I made my way back to Inga's in high spirits. I felt certain our scheme could not fail. When I arrived I was greeted by an enthusiastic dog that barked at me and leaped up on my legs so that I could do nothing but pick him up and carry him. The doctor was sitting in the living room, and for a moment I thought there might be bad news, but he assured me that this was an entirely social visit. He had met Inga's mother, who had invited him to go to the opera with her. He had given his regrets, and she had gone on her own.

"How are things going?" he asked.

"Wonderfully," I replied. "I have gone into the real estate business and things are going very well indeed." I was about to tell him of our new venture into apartment blocks, but at the last moment I decided it would probably be best if I kept that quiet until things had gone a little further.

The doctor did not seem interested beyond merely passing the time, and we turned to other topics. We were discussing the last election when Inga came into the room.

"So Dalgleish welcomed you, did he?" she asked. The dog in the meanwhile was squirming to get out of my arms. I set him down on the floor and he immediately ran barking to Inga.

"Good dog," she said, stooping to pat him, though nothing he had done seemed worthy of the praise. "Can you take him for a walk? I'd do it, but I'm in the middle of making supper."

"I'll do it," the doctor said. "I was just going for a walk myself and I could use the company." He stood up from the chesterfield and Inga handed him the leash. The dog was pleased, and practically dragged the doctor out the door.

Inga walked into the kitchen and I followed her. The setting sun shone horizontally through the window, and in the brilliant golden light Inga looked particularly beautiful. She was wearing a dark green skirt and a white blouse with tiny flowers printed on it. She smelled faintly of perfume, and as she brushed against me I was struck by desire. Without thinking of the consequences, I took her in my arms and kissed her. She kissed me back, then drew away and said, "That's a surprise. It's exactly what my father warned me about. But I didn't think you were interested. I thought you had a love of your life and nothing else would do."

"I think I might be falling in love with you," I told her, though the idea was so new that I couldn't be sure of what I was saying.

"Well, let's not rush into anything until you're more certain. I am going to the Normal School and I don't want anything to prevent me from getting my teacher's licence. And that's going to take me a full year." I kissed her again and apologized. She went back to her cooking and I went to my room to ponder what I had done.

The weeks that followed allowed me plenty of time to ponder. I practised my guitar, learned many new songs and fell into a sort of dull domesticity so that each day was similar to the day before. The summer cooled, birds began to fly south and the leaves on the trees turned yellow and scarlet and brown. Inga's mother was finding the city less exciting than she had expected. She missed her neighbours and was finding it hard to make new friends.

I made another trip to Toronto with Johnny and we met with Hawkins. He had drawn up contracts for us to sign, and we were to start on building our first apartment block. Everything, he said, was working as smoothly as it could. I remembered then that I had not met with the Icelanders who we were counting on to be our workers, and I resolved to escape my lethargy and get back to work as soon as we returned.

I looked for Lara, of course. I went back to the Bishop Strachan School and waited for her to appear. I recognized some of the students from my last visit, but I didn't see Lara. Then on the last evening before we were due to depart, Johnny and I went to Massey Hall to hear the Mendelssohn Choir under the direction of August Vogt. We had heard of this magnificent new opera house and wanted to see it as much for the architecture as for the music. And it was magnificent. Winnipeg's opera house was a theatre that presented everything from comic revues and plays to lectures and boxing matches. This theatre was constructed for large musical presentations, and the choir was the best I had ever heard. There were seventy-five performers, and though I had not heard of any of the composers except Mendelssohn, the music was wonderful.

At the intermission we went out into the hallway for a smoke. I heard a voice that I immediately recognized, and turned to see Lara dressed in a midnight blue evening gown and leaning on the arm of a tall, slender man in a formal black suit. She caught sight of me and beckoned me over. She introduced the man as Robin Blackpole and casually mentioned that he was her fiancé. I congratulated them both, though I did not feel particularly happy about the relationship. She introduced me as a childhood friend, and he gave me a look that implied that my friendship with Lara could now be regarded as historical. I asked her whether she would be returning to Winnipeg in the near future, and to my surprise she answered yes, she would be back in Winnipeg in about a month, and perhaps we could get together for a cup of coffee. Her fiancé gave me a dark look and, saying that the intermission was ending, hurried her away to their seats.

The train trip back to Winnipeg gave me plenty of time to ponder, but I could not come to any conclusion. Apparently I was in love with two women and did not wish to give either of them up. The situation was clearly impossible, but that didn't help me to plan my future at all. The only plan I could make was to try to keep all of my options open and just see what happened. Lara was to be married, but something made me think that the wedding was only one of a series of possible futures, and not the most likely.

As soon as I was back in Winnipeg I went out to find the Icelanders who worked for the railway. I found Siggi and Villi at the railway station, but Thor had gone back to Hecla. Their English was little better than it had been when they first came to Winnipeg. I asked them how they liked their jobs, and they answered that they hated the jobs, but the pay was good and so they had to continue to work until they had enough money to build a house.

"Do you like to build?" I asked them. They both replied that they would much sooner build than work on the railway. I offered them jobs building an apartment block. They were a little suspicious.

"Where does a young man like you get enough money to build an apartment block?" Siggi asked. I told them that Toronto was full of rich Englishmen who wanted to invest in Winnipeg. I told them about Johnny and I asked if they knew other Icelanders who wanted work. I told them that the language on the job would be Icelandic, and that the pay would be higher than they got on the railway. I asked them to talk to any other Icelanders they knew who could build, and told them to meet me at Inga's house on the evening of the following Thursday. I would have contracts for them and a week's wages in advance. We shook hands, and I left them to think over the offer.

That afternoon I told Johnny of my plan.

"Many workers in the city have gone on strike lately," he said.

"The Icelanders will not strike against us if they are allowed to speak Icelandic," I said. "They will be loyal and hard-working. If we give them a week's wages in advance, they will be convinced that they are in good hands with us."

Johnny thought my idea was good, but he had some doubts. Who would be the foreman? How would we communicate with the workers?

I reminded him that I could speak perfectly good Icelandic, and that I would like to spend time at the site working with the men.

The following Thursday, Johnny and I waited at Inga's house for the Icelanders. Inga had gone out for a rehearsal with the Unitarian

Church choir. Siggi and Villi arrived at the door at about eight in the evening. They brought six other men with them. Apparently they had all been working on the railway, but all were more than willing to take me up on my offer. One by one, we shook hands with them, and I passed each man a cheque. Johnny had wanted me to ask them to sign contracts, but I told him that they would be insulted if we did. The Icelanders regarded a man's word as better than any written contract.

I offered everyone a glass of beer and a cigar. Only two of the men drank, but they all took the cigar. I made coffee for the rest, and each man told his story. All were from the north of Iceland, from Eyjafjordur district. All claimed to be excellent carpenters, and when we began construction a week later that proved no idle boast. Johnny arrived with the architect, a man named Charles Wheeler, and with the plans, and my men set to work immediately. I was surprised to find that half of them were able to read blueprints.

And Lara arrived in Winnipeg as she had promised. I found a note addressed to me in the mailbox. The envelope was perfumed, and the invitation inside was written in the Palmer method, the letters joined together and carefully scripted so that the words seemed to flow. The newspapers had written about this revolutionary new method of writing, and though I had seen several words written out in the article, it was the first time I had actually seen an entire sentence.

The invitation requested my company "at the home of Gudmundur Palsson on the eleventh inst. dress informal and dinner and an evening of music. RSVP." I replied in as elegant a hand as I could manage, informing my host that I would certainly attend and thanking him for his kindness in thinking of me. I carried it over to Gudmundur's house and placed it in the mailbox. Back on the street, I looked up at Lara's window. Her room was brightly lit, but though I waited for about a half-hour, Lara did not appear.

The days before the eleventh I spent preparing for the building of the apartment block. There was plenty to do. We had to prepare the ground, haul in gravel and bricks and lumber and begin to construct a foundation. The weather continued to be fine and our workers seemed happy, speaking Icelandic.

Inga seemed content with her studies. She worked diligently every evening, and I was tired enough that I was willing to play my music for an hour or so every evening and head off to bed early. The walking of the dog had fallen to me by default, and it was usually the last thing I did before I went to bed. One night I arrived back early and so took Dalgleish for his walk before dark. He didn't like to be leashed, so I usually just let him romp. Sometimes he escaped and I couldn't find him, but he was always home by the next morning. This time he was reluctant to leave the yard. He ran to a small clump of trees in the garden and began to bark. A small squirrel darted out of the shrubbery and ran to a nearby tree. Dalgleish ran after it, barking, though he didn't seem to want to catch it. Then suddenly, the squirrel turned and ran after Dalgleish, chasing him up onto the verandah. They played this game for several minutes until the squirrel climbed up into the branches of a tree and sat there, preening itself.

When I took the dog back into the house, I told Inga about this strange behaviour.

"That's Gretta," she said. "She sits in the branches of the tree and watches me put on makeup every morning. She's a very smart squirrel. Dalgleish always sits beside me when I am at my dresser, and he barks at her. I think they've become friends."

"It's a kind of unlikely friendship," I answered. "Dogs rarely make friends with squirrels."

"All's fair in love and war," Inga answered, and left me to ponder the implications of her reply.

On the eleventh, I arrived at the Gudmundur Palsson mansion, dressed for a formal occasion. There were eight of us altogether: Gudmundur, Lara, Gregory, Monsieur Dorge, myself, three people I did not know, and to my surprise, Johnny. It soon became clear that a tall young woman with raven black hair would provide the music, accompanied by Monsieur Dorge.

"I'd like you to meet Halldor and Lilja," Lara announced, introducing the new couple. "They are my cousins from Iceland, here for a visit." Halldor was a tall man with prematurely white hair, dressed in a black suit. Lilja was also tall with red hair that was nearly orange. I spoke to them in Icelandic, welcoming them to Winnipeg, but they responded in an accented but clear English.

"We wish to practise our English," Lilja said. "We are not here for long, so we must speak as much English as we can. There will be plenty of opportunity to speak Icelandic at home."

"Halldor is looking for business opportunities in Canada,"

Gudmundur explained. "He owns several businesses in Iceland, and the best stable of horses in the country."

Halldor smiled as if to demur, but he went on to say that he would match his horses against anyone else's. I had taken them to be husband and wife, but it soon became clear that they were brother and sister. I had expected that we would be offered wine, but we were left to chat without refreshment.

A gong sounded and we filed into the dining room. There was a small piano in a corner of the room, and Monsieur Dorge sat down at it. The young woman with the very black hair picked up some music from the top of the piano. The rest of us sat at the table while Monsieur Dorge introduced the woman as Miss Hemphill, a soprano from Toronto who would be giving a concert at the opera house next week.

Monsieur Dorge struck a few notes on the piano, and Miss Hemphill began to sing in a light, melodious voice. The songs were all from Italian light opera, she explained. I had never heard any of the music before, but it was pleasant. She sang for about fifteen minutes, and we all clapped our hands when they finished. Then she and Monsieur Dorge bowed and left the room. They did not rejoin us for dinner.

Lara was in fine spirits. She amused everyone with tales about her escapades at the Bishop Strachan School, though she kept her stories at a level that would not frighten a father. Johnny was seated next to Lilja. They spoke together in whispers and I could not make out what they said, though they both laughed a lot. Halldor told of their trip here by sea. They had been in excellent quarters, though many of the immigrants on the ship had been ill, and one baby had died on the way over.

Supper was a venison roast, with vegetables cooked in a sauce that was very tasty. We ate saskatoon berry pie for dessert, though we were still not offered wine. When everyone had finished, Gudmundur invited the men to join him in his study for brandy and cigars. Lara and her cousin Lilja went into a room she called the parlour and they said they would join us later.

When we men had all been served our brandy and lit our cigars, Gudmundur proposed a toast to Winnipeg, and we all chimed in. Gudmundur said that any man of intelligence and spirit could make a fortune here, and he proposed a second toast to Johnny and me.

"These young men," he told Halldor, "have at a very young age succeeded in business in a manner that would be a model for many of the elder businessmen of this province." Then turning to me, he added, "I speak of course of your plans for an apartment block. And though I admire your acumen, I must inform you that you will soon have competition. Already several of my acquaintances are having their own plans drawn up for more apartment blocks."

"There will be room for many," I responded.

"Yes," Gudmundur answered. "But a good idea is good for only a short while. Then everyone knows about it and it is not so easy."

"It's a question of market strategy," Johnny replied. "Who is to live in these apartments? The one who guesses that will be the one who makes money."

"And who do you think that will be?"

"The working man," Johnny replied. "The carpenter who builds the apartments, the plumber and the mason. They have both the need and the money. I know of several plans for apartments that are doomed because they are built for rich men. But rich men live in houses, not apartments."

I was a little concerned that Johnny was giving away too many of our secrets, but Gudmundur simply nodded and said, "We shall see."

Halldor had followed our conversation carefully, and he now said, "I am very impressed with you young men. I had asked Gudmundur to put me in touch with some bright young businessmen. I wonder if you would be willing to meet with me in a few days to discuss some propositions?"

Johnny agreed at once, and we planned to meet at the café near the railway station in three days. Then we all trooped into the parlour to meet the ladies. I managed to get Lara aside and ask what her fiancé was doing while she was here.

"He is no longer my fiancé," she told me. "My father has forbidden the wedding, which is fine with me, because he was becoming a bore. I am to be sent to Iceland to stay with Halldor and Lilja for six months so that my broken heart can recover. I am careful to let my father know that I am distraught but a dutiful daughter. And so I will holiday in Iceland."

"Will I see you before you leave?"

"That will be up to you. I am here for another week. If you are brave enough to come to my father's house, then you will see me."

After a few desultory conversations, we broke up, and I found myself walking down the street with Johnny.

"Do you remember when you told me that you had fallen hopelessly in love?"

"Yes."

"Well, I didn't know what you meant at the time, but I do now. I am hopelessly in love with Lilja."

"That was quick. Does she share your feelings?"

"I don't know. But I will know tomorrow. I am taking her out for dinner."

"Be careful. It will be hard to conduct a relationship with her in Iceland and you in Winnipeg."

"I'll find a way," he said, and he left me there at the door to Inga's house. I waited a moment, then entered to the joyful barking of the dog.

The next couple of days I worked with the men setting the foundation. It was hard physical work, but I enjoyed it. The men were excavating the mud from the basement of the block with scoops pulled by horses. The ground was hard, and the men had to stop often to rest the horses. Wagons loaded with rocks arrived and we piled them near the sidewalk.

That evening, I worked up my courage and knocked on

Gudmundur's door. Lara answered the door and let me in. She was wearing a white dress that looked as if it might have been a nightgown, except that she wore a brooch that glittered with some bright blue stones that I did not recognize. She had on a gold locket in the shape of a heart, and she looked cool and confident.

"So," she said, "have you come to talk to me about the great love affair?"

"Which affair is that?" I asked.

"Lilja and Johnny, of course. He has quite stolen her heart. She can hardly bear to be out of his company."

"I understand the feeling is mutual," I told her. "But almost certainly doomed since they live in different countries with a wide ocean between them."

"Not so wide anymore. It is more money than distance that keeps them apart. And since you have both become wealthy entrepreneurs, it should not be difficult."

"We will not be wealthy for long if we do not stay in Winnipeg and take care of our building. In fact, we will soon be bankrupt if we don't supervise things carefully." As I spoke, Lara walked over to a sideboard against the wall, and she opened a door and took out a bottle of gin and a bottle of whisky. She raised her eyebrows to ask whether I would join her in a drink, and I nodded in reply.

"Where is your father?" I asked.

"Gone to Grand Forks on business. And he has taken Gregory with him, so I am all alone." She poured the drinks and we clinked our glasses as if we were going to toast something.

"I am afraid things will be dry in Iceland. The Knights Templar are strong there and there will probably be prohibition soon. Apparently nearly everyone disapproves of alcohol."

"You will be with Halldor and Lilja. How do they feel about drinking?"

"I don't know about Halldor, but Lilja was quite ready to have a nip the other night after you left. But come, I have something to show you." She led me up to the music room and showed me a strange machine she called an Edison Standard Phonograph. It was a metal contraption in a wooden box, and it had a large trumpet. Lara took a wax cylinder from a shelf where it stood with several others. She put it in the machine, then moved an arm with a needle so that it sat on the cylinder. The machine had a crank on its side, and as she cranked it began to play music. I was astonished. I had never seen anything like it. I listened while the machine played a march, which took about two minutes. Then she put on another cylinder, and asked me to dance. We stood there in each other's arms, swaying to the music, and I could smell her perfume and feel her soft body.

"Where did you get this?" I asked.

"My father bought it in New York City," she said. "He believes that in a short time everyone will want to own one, and he wants to be the one who sells them in Canada."

"He's right," I said. "Especially if they come with beautiful girls who will dance with you."

"You'll have to find your own beautiful girls, but I suppose you will have no problem with that."

She had brought her bottle of gin with her, and she poured herself another drink. I had finished my whisky and I allowed her to fill my glass with gin.

"What was the matter with your fiancé?" I asked.

"He was possessive and self-important, but worst of all, he was boring. He could talk about nothing but money. And he gave himself airs. He thought a poor little Icelandic girl should be grateful that a high Anglican like himself would deign to court her. He was full of romantic notions about how he would save me from Iceland, but he'll soon get over it. He'll marry some Toronto girl whose family will have enough money so that he doesn't have to worry. I think probably he was more in love with my father, or at least my father's money, than he was with me. And there is likely some other problem, since my father has forbidden me from seeing him. I don't know what it is, but it must certainly have something to do with money."

Lara put another cylinder on the phonograph, and we danced again, continuing to dance long after the song had ended. Then she took me by the hand and led me to her room in the tower. We made love and she fell asleep immediately. I lay in bed awake for hours wondering about where my life was likely to take me.

In the morning I awoke alone, but I found her in the dining room eating oatmeal porridge. We did not discuss the night before. She told me that she would be leaving for Montreal in a couple of days, and that I would not see her again until she returned from Iceland. I asked her whether I should wait for her.

"As you like," she said. "But I promise nothing."

"Good," I answered. "Then I will make no promises either."

I began to enjoy working with the men, and as the days passed and summer turned to fall and then to winter, I found myself up early and home to bed late. Inga was busy studying to become a teacher, and I did not see much of her. I walked Dalgleish most nights before I went to bed. Johnny was distant and distracted. He was continually making plans to go to Iceland, and he included me in his plans because he did not speak the language and needed me as a guide.

The brother wrote from Vancouver. He had married Elin against her parent's wishes, and they were living in a couple of rooms in a rooming house. He had a job as a fisherman, and Elin was doing housework, though she would soon have to quit because she was going to have a baby. I wrote back to congratulate him, and sent twenty dollars for the baby.

The letter reminded me that I had not been back to New Iceland for months. We had slowed construction because the winter was particularly cold and it snowed almost every day, and it seemed a good time to go. I put Siggi and Villi in charge of the building site, and told the other Icelanders to go home and come back in six weeks. They seemed pleased to have some time off, and I gave each of them a small bonus.

I told Inga about my plans to visit New Iceland, and invited her to join me. She said she could come for only a few days because she had to go to her classes, but I convinced her a short break would do her good, so she agreed.

We took the coach to Gimli on a Thursday and we planned to return on the following Tuesday. There was a strange cloud formation in the shape of an arch to the west, and the light was oddly orange. By the time we reached Selkirk, a light snowfall had begun. It had been cold for the past two weeks, but the temperature was milder now. Still, something in the air seemed ominous, and by the time we reached Boundary Creek, the wind had begun to howl, and the driver could no longer see where he was going. He said there was no hope of getting to Gimli that day, and we drove to the Boundary Creek Hotel, which had just opened.

Our host introduced himself as Captain Baldi Anderson. He was a small but athletic man who wore a captain's hat. He had only one room left in the hotel, and so we took it. I was surprised to see that a hotel had opened in Boundary Creek, but the Captain explained the railway would soon arrive, and with it hundreds of city dwellers looking for holidays. The place would be humming in no time. I had heard a railway was to be built, but I had no idea that it had progressed so far.

The Captain took us to his dining room and offered Inga a glass of gin and me a glass of brandy. Inga declined the gin, but I accepted the proffered brandy and in return offered him a cigar, which he was pleased to accept. He had just come back from Alaska, he told us. He had gone there to study methods of cattle farming, and he was now filled with new ideas about how to raise cattle in New Iceland. He told stories until Inga excused herself and went to our room.

I told him about our apartment building and he was very excited. He said if we planned to build another block, he would be interested in investing in it. I told him about my adventures as a shoeshine boy, and it turned out that he too had been a shoeshine boy many years ago. He took me outside and showed me his dogs. They were chained out in the howling blizzard. He said he had the best dog team anywhere in the Great Northwest. He had a plan for bringing the dog team to Winnipeg and offering people rides in Central Park for twenty-five cents a ride. He said he believed in taking advantage of whatever situation he found, and instead of complaining about winter, we should see it as an opportunity to make money.

It was well after midnight when I stumbled off to bed. Inga was asleep in the bed, and since the room was small and there was nowhere else to lie down, I climbed into the bed with her. I woke once during the night to find my arm around her and her hair in my face. She smelled of perfume and her breath was sweet. Outside, the wind howled.

When we awoke the next morning the blizzard was over. The snow lay in deep drifts, but the wind had dropped and the day was clear and sunny. The coachman had taken his coach and gone back to Winnipeg, but the Captain said the he would take us to Gimli by dog team. He and one of his workers were going there anyway, and we were welcome to come along for the ride.

I had never ridden behind a dog team before, nor had Inga. We set out over the frozen lake and we arrived in less than an hour. The Captain dropped us off at Thorkelsson's general store. I walked Inga to her father's house, then continued on to my parents' place. It was quieter than I expected, because most of the children were at school. My father was not home. I had not informed anyone that I was coming, and so he had gone to Husavik to get some nets. My mother offered me coffee and fresh doughnuts and I accepted.

"Have you heard from your brother?" she asked.

"Yes. He is in Vancouver with his wife. He is working as a fisherman, and they are expecting a child."

"He never writes. I hear of him only from her parents. They moved back here after the marriage. They don't like him, so they don't tell me much. Why did he have to go to Vancouver?"

"He says the weather is better there. And he earns more money than he could here. Though everything there is expensive." My mother looked very tired and I said as much.

"Yes," she answered. "I am very tired. Your father works hard but he also spends a lot of money, and I have to raise the children by myself. Since Flora left I have had little help. And now your sister wants to go to Winnipeg to work. She says there is no future for a young person in New Iceland, and she uses you as an example."

"Does our father drink too much?" I asked.

"Sometimes. But he is never mean. He just gets happy and sings and teases the children. They love him when he is drunk. When he is sober he broods about money, but when he is drunk he gives away whatever money he has."

"We will have to find help for you," I said. "We will find a live-in girl, and I will pay her wages. We always had girls when I was small."

"Will you also find her another room and a bed?"

"Yes," I told her. "I will do that."

"I have nieces in Libau who would come. I don't think you have met many of your aunts and uncles."

"Father told me that you had five sisters. I met Gudrun and her husband Halli in Selkirk. But they have no children."

"No," she answered. "Halli got the mumps soon after they were married and now he cannot have children. But my sister Benna in Libau has two sons and five daughters. Perhaps one of the girls would come for at least a while. She could sleep in Asta's bed if Asta goes to Winnipeg."

"What will Asta do in Winnipeg?"

"She says she will go and live with you. Apparently she can get a job at the Mackenzie and Powis warehouse on Princess Street."

"Does she have a job there?"

"She has written to them, and they have asked her to come in for an interview." I must admit I hadn't suspected my sister of having such an enterprising streak. I remembered her mostly as a child, but she was certainly now a young woman. As for her coming to live with me, that might take some thinking.

My father did not come home until after dark. Nor did Asta. The younger children burst in just after four, filling the house with noise. The younger girls seemed afraid of me at first, but after a few minutes they ignored me as if I didn't exist. Asta and my father arrived together, dressed in parkas and ushering in the cold from outside. I greeted them, and they welcomed me. Asta was the first to speak.

"I have to talk to you, Baldur," she said. "I am going to Winnipeg to get a job and I have no place to stay, so can I stay with you?" This was a little more forthright than I had expected, but I could see only one possible response.

"You may stay with me for a while, but once you have your job and you are earning an income, you will want your own place, or perhaps you will find someone to room with you."

"That's wonderful," she said, and putting her parka on once more, she left the house.

"Where has she gone?" I asked.

"To visit her friends," my father said. "To tease them and to gloat at her good fortune. And meanwhile your poor mother is worked to the bone taking care of children."

"Perhaps she would not be so overworked if you could resist bringing more and more children home for her to raise. I hate the thought of you travelling, because you find children on trains."

My father shrugged. "All the children need care. I cannot see a child who suffers from hunger or poverty if I can do something about it. Besides, your mother does not complain about the children. Only about the work."

"I think I can help there," I said. "Mother's sister Benna has a daughter who would like to come and help out. I will supply a small salary to pay her for her work."

"She will have less work here than at home," my mother said. "I think she would be happy just to get out of Libau and their cramped house."

"No, we must pay her something," my father said. "We do not need charity." We agreed that my mother would write her sister, and with luck the girl could arrive in about a week. We ate the dinner my mother had prepared, boiled sunfish with boiled potatoes and green tomato relish. It was her specialty, and the family ate it every second day. The younger children complained, but my father treated the meal as a special event for which he had long waited. Then we retired to the living room, where my father brought out his bottle of rye whisky and I provided cigars and we settled in for the evening. My mother shepherded the children into their beds, and when they were asleep she returned to the kitchen with her knitting.

I told my father about the apartment block and about our progress. He shrugged and said high finance was something he did not understand. We puffed our meditative cigars until the room was blue with smoke. My mother came in and asked how we could stand to draw such vile-smelling smoke into our lungs. Then she brought us coffee and returned to her knitting.

"What would you think if I decided to go to Iceland?" I asked my father.

"I would think you were mad. I would think that cigar smoke had rotted your brain."

"My partner Johnny is anxious to go. He has fallen in love with a young woman from Iceland and he wishes to see her."

"Then by all means he should go. But surely he can woo her by himself without your help?"

"I'm sure he can. But I would like to see the place myself. I've heard so much about it."

"It is beautiful," my father said, "but it is also bleak and desolate. Many people live in houses made of sod. Even in the summer it is cold. Many people go hungry. No, I have been there, and it is better here. I would never go back. But if you have the time and the money, then it is for you to decide. Just be careful that you don't fall in love in Iceland and have to live there for the rest of your life."

"It is pretty cold here," I told him. "We have just had a terrible blizzard. I hear that their winters are much milder than our own."

"That's true," he said. "But it can be pretty cold in a sod hut even without a blizzard." He thought for a moment. "You are a very lucky man."

"What do you mean?"

"You are like Olaf the Peacock in Laxdaela saga. The world gives you everything you want without much effort. You should be grateful."

"Not everything," I told him. "But I am grateful for what I have."

Our cigars had pretty much burned to small stubs, and my mother was preparing to go to bed, so we said good night and I found my way to the sofa and slept till morning.

My father was already gone when I got up and drank the cup of coffee my mother offered me. She had cooked oatmeal, but I have never much liked it. Still, I ate a few mouthfuls so as not to seem ungrateful. The day was clear and very cold. When I left the house, my breath rose up in a cloud before me. I walked to the graveyard, but the snow was far too deep for any of the voices of the dead to make themselves heard. I whistled the "Ode to Joy" anyway out of some form of nostalgia for my vanished youth.

Asta met me on my way back to the house. She was terribly excited about her impending visit to Winnipeg. She had been there only once before, and I had been in Toronto the days of her visit. Now she had a thousand questions for me about Winnipeg, but the one that surprised me was when she asked me if I intended to marry Inga.

"Everyone thinks you should," she said. "What with the two of you living there alone together, there's a lot of gossip, you know. All the girls were looking at her tummy to see if she was going to have a baby."

"All the girls can mind their own businesses," I told her. "I have no intention of marrying Inga, and she has no intention of marrying me. And her mother is living with us as well. I hope you are not spreading gossip."

"No, of course not," she answered. "But people can't help talking. Have you told Inga that I am coming to stay with you?"

"I haven't seen her since we arrived," I said. "But I will go and talk to her about it now." We had arrived back at the house, and I told her to go in. I would not need her help to speak to Inga. She was disappointed but she went in and I carried on to Inga's father's house. Inga was alone when I arrived there. Her father had gone to Winnipeg to see her mother.

"We should have let my father know we were coming," Inga said. "That would have saved a lot of problems."

I told Inga of Asta's plans, and asked whether she would allow Asta to stay for a few weeks until she got settled.

"I think it will work out just fine," she said. "Especially since it seems that my mother will be coming back to my father's house and there will be an empty room."

"I will pay for her, of course," I said. "But if your mother is gone I would like my old room back again."

"I think she wants to keep it in case she decides to move back. But there is still plenty of room." The sun was bright and it shone in through the living room window and onto the linoleum floor. It also shone on Inga's hair, making her beautiful.

"When are we going back?" she asked me.

"I want to talk to Captain Baldi before we go. I think he will be visiting my father sometime today. But we can go back first thing tomorrow if you want."

"I'd like to catch my parents before they come back to New Iceland."

"The coach will leave at eight o'clock tomorrow," I told her. "That's its usual time, and the storm is over."

She said she would be ready and waiting. Back home I found Asta and told her to get ready to go. If she was coming to Winnipeg, then it was best she go with me and Inga. We didn't want her to get lost.

"I wouldn't get lost," she replied, but she went and packed her bag and went out to tell her friends that she was off on her adventures. I stayed with my mother until noon. We didn't have much to say, but we talked anyway.

After lunch, I walked over to Hans Petur Tergesen's store. It was an impressive building, the newest place in town. My father and the Captain were seated in a couple of old chairs near the stove. The Captain said that he had thought about our conversation, and he'd like to make me a business proposition. He thought he would sell his hotel at Boundary Creek and build a new one in Gimli. The railroad was going to continue on, and he could have it ready by the time the trains arrived. He thought he could sell the Boundary Creek Hotel for enough money to build a new one, and still have enough money to invest in the building boom in Winnipeg. We agreed that I would discuss the matter with my partner Johnny and we would meet in Winnipeg over the summer.

The trip back to Winnipeg was uneventful. The storm was over but the road was covered in deep snow. The coach was cold, but we had buffalo skin robes to keep us warm. It was late afternoon when we arrived, and it was already dusk. Winnipeg was lit with electric lights and the streets looked festive. Shoppers walked around with boxes and bags, and Asta was delighted. She could hardly wait until we were home before she was out to walk in the glowing streets.

The next few weeks were a melancholy time for me. Inga was hard at work studying to be a teacher and so I spent most of my time with Dalgleish, taking him for walks or just reading before the fire with the dog on my lap. There was work to do, of course. There is always work to do, and now that spring was arriving there was plenty to do at the apartment block. The men had become a little lazy during their time off in the winter, but they were soon back with high enthusiasm. Asta was soon hired, as she predicted. Mackenzie and Powis needed girls at their warehouse on Princess Street, and Asta, though normally of a fierce temper, could be charming when she chose. She was hired immediately at her interview and set to work right then.

Asta implored me to buy her a typewriter, a Remington, one of the sort used by Mackenzie and Powis. She was convinced that if she could learn to type with speed she would soon be promoted and would earn enough money to rent her own place. I found one at a reasonable price and brought it home. Asta soon developed a larger social life that left her little time to practise, and by mid-May, she had decided to take rooms with one of the girls at work.

I had been so busy at the apartment that I had not seen Johnny for a long time. That was not unusual and I was not worried, but the same day that Asta moved out I received a telegram from Johnny. He had sent it from Reykjavik. He had gone to Iceland by ship in early May. He said I must come immediately because he had urgent news. He did not say what constituted that urgent news, and though I telegraphed back, I received no reply.

That evening I told Inga that I would be making a visit to Iceland. She was clearly disappointed, but brightened when I told her I would not be gone for long. She too had good news. She had been offered a job teaching small children in the Fort Garry area to the south of Winnipeg, on the condition that she do well in her exams. I congratulated her and wished her luck. That night I took her out to a restaurant for dinner in order to celebrate. I had a bottle of champagne that I had been saving for just such an occasion, and I opened it when we came home. Inga loved the taste of it, and she drank more than she should have. When she was going to bed, she gave me a long lingering kiss, then went into her bedroom and left the door open. I sat up for several more hours but finally went to my own bed, not knowing whether I had made the right decision or not.

The trip to Iceland was disheartening. I will not describe it to you in detail, because it is not something I wish to remember. I took a long train ride to Montreal on a train that kept breaking down. From Montreal I took a ship to Glasgow in raging seas and cold weather with rain. I was sick most of the way. Glasgow was cold and dirty and expensive. The trip to Reykjavik was even worse. By the time I arrived I had lost so much weight that my clothes hung on me as if they belonged to some larger, heartier person.

Still, it was a new country, a place I had never seen before but which inhabited my imagination as if I had been born there. I spoke the language. I could get around as well as I could in Canada. Reykjavik was small, but it was clean and every street looked as if it had recently been washed. I found a hotel and settled in, hoping to meet Johnny, but also hoping more that I would encounter Lara. I did not know where either of them was, but the place was so small I thought I could just walk out into the street and ask their names and someone would tell me where they were. It wasn't even that difficult. I came down from my room hoping to find a meal, and there, standing by the desk, was Johnny.

"About time you arrived," he told me. I've been looking for you every day for a week."

"Well, here I am," I told him, "but if my trip here was what travel to Iceland is like, I expect that this will be my last trip."

"You'll grow to love it," Johnny said. "I've only been here for a month and already I am in love with this place."

"Are you sure it is the place?" I asked him. "I suspected you of other motives."

"Yes, and you are right as always. You are here to stand up for me in my impending marriage to Lilja."

"That's the emergency that made me drop everything and travel here?"

"What could be more important? But, yes, we have business to do as well. I will tell you about it later. Now it is time for you to join me in a bottle of excellent whisky that I bought in Glasgow." He followed me up to my room and opened the bottle and we both drank from the small glasses the landlord had provided.

"How did you find me?" I asked.

"This is the only decent hotel in Reykjavik. You would not stay anywhere else."

Johnny went on to inform me that we would be leaving by boat the next morning for Dalvik. I would stay with the teacher from the farm at Tjorn. The wedding would take place on Saturday in the farm church, and then there would be a party at the local hall. Lara would be there, of course. She would be part of the wedding party, and she was staying with Lilja until the day. By the time Johnny left we had both drunk too much of the good Scotch whisky, and I tumbled into bed to dream of Lara, though in the dream I confused Lara with Inga. When I awoke in the morning I felt anxious and confused, and I vowed that I would resist whisky in the future.

It took two days on a steamboat to reach Dalvik. The boat was a fishing boat, and it smelled of fish and bluestone. But the weather was at last fine, and I watched the puffins and fulmars and shearwaters nesting on the cliffs. They were just at the beginning of the nesting period, and the birds squabbled and cried and rose into the air by the hundreds. I had never seen so many birds at one time. Sometimes we would see men hanging from the cliffs by ropes, robbing the nests of their eggs. It seemed a reckless sort of venture, but we never saw anyone fall.

We were met at the dock by Halldor and Lilja and the teacher Thorarinn Kristjan Eldjarn. Thorarinn was an immense man with shaggy black hair and enormous arms. He did not look much like the blond Icelanders I had encountered in Reykjavik. We loaded our luggage onto a wagon, and we joined it, while the others rode on horses. Those horses were smaller than the ones I had grown up with in New Iceland, but they were very sturdy. I noticed the saddles were set further back on the horses than was the practice in New Iceland, but no one could explain to me why this was. We rode for about a half-hour before we came to the farm. It overlooked the pond at the centre of the valley. Snow-capped mountains were reflected in the pond, and swans swam lazily as if they were tiny icebergs. The air was so clear and the light so intense that the swans were mirrored in the pond. At the far end of the valley a small glacier gleamed an intense white. Johnny told me that he had climbed partway up the mountain on our left, and he had found a small stream where the water ran hot. When we arrived at the farm, a small herd of horses rushed up to greet us, but then decided they would not and they turned and ran past the barn and into the field beyond.

The next few days I spent exploring the area. Thorarinn loaned me a horse, and though I had only occasionally ridden a horse before, I found it quite easy. The horse, whose name was Brunni, was very strong and also very friendly. He was the smoothest horse I had ever ridden, and by the end of the third day I felt like a real horseman. Johnny did not ride with me, but Thorarinn came out for one afternoon. He was practising speaking English and he was remarkably good.

The wedding was to take place in the church at Tjorn. It was a small church with a quite remarkable altarpiece painted by a local artist. The interior was blue and yellow, and the pews were made from oak, which must have been expensive since the country has so few trees. In fact, I saw no trees except for a few stunted birches in all my travels. The graveyard around the church was small, with only a couple of rusted metal crosses and perhaps a dozen stones.

I wondered whether the dead in that churchyard had stories to tell. I gathered that since there were so few Icelanders, you could claim kin with almost any Icelander who had ever lived and be sure the relationship could be discovered. I sat quietly in the graveyard and listened. I imagined voices out of a distant past coming to speak to me, and so I spoke to them. I told them about New Iceland and I told them about my family. I hoped they were listening.

The next day the bridal party arrived dressed in national costume, the women in full-length black-and-white dresses and the men in simple black suits. The guests began to file in, and though the church was small, there was no large crowd. Once the audience had taken its seats, Johnny and I entered and stood at the front of the church on the right-hand side. Then Lilja and Lara and two other women came in and joined us on the other side. The ceremony was short and simple and we were done in less than a half-hour. Johnny and Lilja and the women left in one wagon. Thorarinn and Halldor and I followed in a second wagon.

There were far more people at the party than there had been at the church. Women were bustling around carrying platters of food and steaming jugs of coffee. The hall was quite large. And a small band of musicians was warming up on a stage at the far end. People seated themselves at tables and chatted away. As soon as I could, I made my way over to Lara.

"So you came," she said to me.

"Yes," I said. "I appear to have done that."

"Was it a terrible journey?" she asked.

"Yes," I said. "Very terrible."

"It always is. It never gets any better. The sea is cold and windy and the waves are awful. You must be a very good friend to do this for Johnny."

"If I had known what the trip was going to be like I probably would not have come. But I am here now, and I intend to make the best of it."

"Are you looking for adventure?"

"If it comes my way," I told her. "This is a new country that I am unlikely ever to see again. And so yes, I would like an adventure."

"Some of us are going across the mountain pass to Kolbeinsdalur and on to Holar. We will spend one day in Holar and then come back."

"What is in Holar?"

"A church. Holar was the capital of the country in the medieval period."

"Then I will certainly join you."

Lara excused herself. As a member of the wedding party, she had obligations. I too had obligations, but these turned out mostly to be smuggling some whisky into Johnny's coffee from a small flask he had handed me just before the wedding. I remembered the other night when we had drunk a bit more than we should have, and so I avoided the whisky.

I managed to get Lara alone for a few minutes and I asked her about the arrangements for the trek. She said that Thorarinn would make all the arrangements. All I had to do was to be up by eight o'clock and dressed for riding. I said I'd be ready, and at that point the party began to break up and I made my way back to my room.

The next morning was bright and clear. Thorarinn had brought the horses to the highest farm in the valley a couple of days before, and we met there to begin the trek. Lara was there along with one of the other women from the wedding party, a tall blonde named Helga, and Halldor. I asked if Johnny and Lilja would join us, but Lara said that they had other plans. The men began to saddle the horses when Thorarinn discovered that one of the horses had lost a shoe. We waited about an hour while he borrowed another shoe from the old farmer who owned the farm where we had gathered. He had a hammer and a few nails, and soon had the horse shod.

We rode the horses towards the pass, and crossed through a barbed-wire gate. In a small corral on the other side were another five horses. Thorarinn set them free and we set out along the narrow trail that led to the mountain pass. All along the way were small cairns made from rock, and they guided us along the trail. Thorarinn told me these markers had been there for a thousand years, and the ancient Icelanders had used them to guide themselves from one valley to the next.

We were moving at a fair clip, and I began to sense I was not the accomplished horseman I had fancied myself. I tried to slow my horse, but apparently horses in Iceland were not taught any language for "stop" or even for "slow." I gave up trying to control the horse and spent my time trying not to fall off. Everyone else seemed completely comfortable. There was almost no conversation because the clatter of the horses' hooves on the rocks drowned out all sound. As we climbed, the paths became narrower, and soon we could see clouds below us. After about two hours of travel, we came to a field of snow. We stopped while Halldor explained there had been an unusual late snowstorm a week ago. He had thought it would have melted by now, and he asked if we wanted to continue. The vote was unanimous to go on.

The snow was deep and the horses had difficulty lunging through it. We had to get off and lead them through the deepest parts. About an hour later we came to a large cairn where there was a clear open rock ledge where we could rest the horses. The other five horses had followed us along, and Thorarinn and Halldor caught them one by one and changed the saddles from the horses we had been riding. We opened a lunch that the women had packed, roast lamb sandwiches and lukewarm coffee, but it tasted very good.

From where we stood, we could see back down to the valley we had left. We could see the shapes of fields, but we were too high to make out individual buildings. Ahead of us stretched a valley to our left and another to the right. Thorarinn announced that we would follow the valley to our left, and we would soon be out of the snow. Halldor turned to the valley to the left and began to sing in a deep baritone. He said he had sung the anthem of the valley, and that it was the practice to sing it whenever you crossed over the highest point in the pass, whichever way you were going.

The slope down was steep and we were soon out of the snow and moving along an ancient path. We crossed several fast-flowing shallow streams with brilliant ducks swimming against the current,

Thorarinn said that they were harlequin ducks. They seemed to be the only birds at that altitude. After riding down several slopes that I thought were far too steep for the horses, we arrived at a marshy area that was flat, but spongy. The horses laboured over the swampy ground, and suddenly my horse broke through the floating grass that looked like firm ground and I was thrown forward onto the ground. The others stopped but it was clear that they could not come to my rescue because their horses too would sink. I managed to get to my feet and caught the bridle. The horse made several lunges and we finally made it to solid ground. I remounted and continued on as if nothing had happened, but my shoulder was sore, and I was certain that I would be very stiff before morning.

A short while later, we reached the long flat bottom of Kolbeinn's Valley. We stopped to change horses again at a stone corral that had once been used for sheep.

I spoke briefly with Lara while the men changed the saddles and examined the horses' hooves. She was concerned that I might have been injured, but I assured her I would be fine. I asked her where we would stay the night, and she told me there were small huts at Holar that could be rented for a reasonable amount of money. We would stay there for two nights, then return to Dalvik. I asked her how she was enjoying her stay in Iceland.

"It's all right," she said. "You get used to it. It always rains and is often cold, but the people are hospitable."

"Are you anxious to get home to Canada?"

"Yes and no."

"What does that mean?"

"Whatever you take it to mean." And she ran over to the next corral to find her horse.

A couple of hours later after we forded a deep river where the horses had to swim, we arrived at Holar. It had a large stone church, the bishop's residence, a school and a number of barns. The main school building had a kitchen that served us a meal of roasted lamb with potatoes and rhubarb sauce. After the day's travel, it was a welcome feast. Several young Icelanders gathered in the room after we had finished eating and they began to sing. I joined in with them and for a couple of hours we sang almost every song I knew. Lara did not sing. She said she had difficulty carrying a tune and that it embarrassed her to sing in public.

When the singing was over, we made our way to the huts. I thought I would be paired with one of the men, but Lara led me to the farthest hut. I was surprised she would make it so obvious that she intended to sleep with me, but none of the others seemed concerned and so I followed her. As soon as we had closed the door, she moved into my arms and kissed me passionately. I did as much for her and for several minutes we stayed that way, tangled in each other's arms. Then she sat on the bed, pulled a bottle of gin from her bag, and offered me a drink. I took it cautiously, but I was stiff from the hours of riding and my fall, and it relaxed me.

"I may marry," she said to me, and took another long draw on the bottle of gin.

"Who do you intend to marry?"

"I have not yet decided, but I have had several offers."

"Why don't you marry me?"

"I don't think it is in the cards. At least not yet. Thorarinn has asked me to marry him."

"The teacher?"

"Yes."

"Won't he be jealous if we spend the night together?"

"He may be or he may not. Icelandic men are strange that way. They are not very jealous."

"Well, I guess a western Icelander is different from the real thing, because I would certainly be jealous under the same circumstances."

"Let's not talk about serious matters," Lara said, "let's dance instead."

For a long time we held each other and swayed in that small hut with a sod roof and the smell of wet grass mixing with her perfume. Then we went into the bed together and lay there for several hours before we made love. Lara fell asleep almost immediately after, but I lay awake wondering, as I so often did, what the world had in store for me.

The following day, we slept late and missed breakfast. In the afternoon Lara and I rode to a little fishing village named Hofsos. We bought some fish from one of the fishermen to take back to the school for supper. The village seemed neat and prosperous, and there was a lot of activity in the harbour, boats coming and going and fishermen unloading their catch. In a field behind the village, thousands of terns were nesting and their sound was nearly deafening. They soared and dived at us as we rode by. We arrived back in the late afternoon and presented our contribution of cod and perch to the school kitchen, and were promised that it would be cooked for dinner.

Halldor caught up to me at dinner and wanted to talk to me. He asked whether Johnny had told me of the business he wanted to conduct with us. I told him that Johnny had been too busy getting married to discuss anything.

"Well, I think I should let you know that Johnny wants to start a business in Iceland. His idea is that you will find some of the newest inventions and sell them in Iceland before anyone else."

"I don't know," I said. "I don't know much about what would sell in Iceland and the only real connections I have are in real estate, and that real estate is in Winnipeg. But I will talk with Johnny and see what he means." Then we shook hands as if we had agreed to something, and Halldor went off to his hut.

The night with Lara was much like the one before. We drank some gin and talked for a long time. I asked Lara if she had thought any more about marriage. She said that she thought she might never marry, but since she was impulsive, she would probably marry some-one and regret it later.

"Are you coming back to Canada?" I asked her again, and she still didn't know. We clung together that night as if we were children who were being separated and who were desperately afraid.

The next morning Lara was again cool and aloof. We rode out from Holar early in the morning and followed the same path back. The horses sensed their return and were anxious and restless. The extra horses who had kept near to us on the way over now took their own way, and we could see them in the distance. I thought we would not be able to catch them to change horses, but Thorarinn told me that when we stopped, they would return to us, and that happened just as he said.

The first part of the trip was harder than the previous trip. The snow was still deep and the way difficult. Once we had passed the cairn that marked the summit, things changed rapidly. The horses sensed we were nearing home, and they galloped without pause, so that I could do nothing but hang on and hope I would not fall off. At the speed we were going a fall would have been disastrous.

Still, nothing happened. We reached the highest farm, changed horses and continued on to the farm at Tjorn. Johnny and Lilja were there, and they were full of questions about our adventure, and full of memories of their own wedding. As seemed to be the practice in Iceland, the evening turned into another singing session. When we went to bed at midnight, it was still bright, the sun just dipping down to touch the horizon. I wanted to talk to Lara, but there was little chance. The next morning I found a letter addressed to me at my place at the table. It was from Lara, and it apologized for not saying goodbye in person. She said she hoped we might meet again in the future, either in Canada or in Iceland.

I returned to Canada a few days later. Johnny and Lilja were on the same ship to Glasgow, but I went on ahead of them to Canada. They wanted to take a short honeymoon in Scotland, and I wanted to get back as soon as I could.

When I arrived back, the apartment block was far behind schedule. For the next few weeks I worked from dawn to dusk getting things in order. People were anxious to move in, and I had rented all the apartments before the building was complete. Many more people wanted apartments than we could accommodate, and it seemed certain we could build as many blocks as we could finance. I had left the finances to Johnny in the past, but now I decided that I would have to take part. Johnny and Lilja had stayed longer in Scotland than they had planned, and so I had to get along without Johnny's advice.

I sent a telegram to Robert Hawkins telling him of the success of our apartment venture and inviting him to Winnipeg to see it. A week later he arrived and in a half day he made contact with investors in Toronto, and we had financing for another block. Johnny arrived back just in time to sign the contract and he was amazed that I had made the financial arrangements. We decided that we would build another block identical to the one we had just built, because we knew all the possible problems, and we knew how to get the thing done on time.

I had hardly spoken to Inga since my return. She was writing her final exams, and was very busy. We passed in hallways from time to time, but that was all. Even the little dog seemed to have forgotten who I was, but once I had some time to breathe and had taken him for a couple of walks he brightened up and stopped growling at me.

I felt like celebrating the completion of the apartment block and the contract for the second one. Inga had received her marks from the normal school, and had led her class. I invited her out for dinner and she accepted. We went to a new restaurant that specialized in French cooking and was run by a little man with a thin moustache and a big white cook's hat. I ordered champagne again, and though Inga swore that she had no intention of drinking too much as she had the previous celebration, we soon ordered a second bottle, and when we got home we were both weaving our way up the stairs. I leaned over and kissed Inga goodnight, and she responded with passion. Before we were really aware of what we were doing, we were both in the same bed, and sometime during that night I asked her to marry me.

It was clear we were going to have to go to Gimli to tell our parents. We caught the coach the next morning, and by evening we were there. We should probably have taken the train that was now operating, but I felt the coach was a more romantic choice. The trip was uneventful, except that a large black bear wandered into the road near Boundary Creek, and he showed no signs of leaving. The driver tried to frighten him away, but he would not be frightened. We waited for several minutes before the bear walked off into the bush. The horses were terrified, and as soon as we started again, they burst into a gallop that threatened to overturn the coach. The driver held tightly to the reins and after a few minutes the horses tired and resumed their usual trot.

Inga thought that the arrival of the bear was some sort of sign, but I convinced her that we had nothing to worry about. There were plenty of bears in the area, and they were almost always benign. If we were to receive messages from some hidden world, then they would be delivered by something other than bears.

We told Inga's parents first. They seemed pleased and congratulated us warmly. The mayor insisted we have a large wedding and invite the entire town. We hadn't discussed the matter, but I had hoped for a quiet reception in the house in Winnipeg. I said that we hadn't made any decisions about the wedding, but we would let them know as soon as we had made plans.

My parents were equally pleased. My mother insisted that she had expected this announcement for some time, and that it was no surprise to her. The children were enthusiastic. They wanted the wedding to take place in Winnipeg so that they could travel to the city and share in the bright lights. The youngest girls wanted to carry flowers and be part of the wedding party. Within a few minutes they were dressing up and rehearsing their parts.

Inga and I both stayed at her parents' place. There was no room at my parents' place because the last bed had been filled by the cousin from Libau who was helping my mother. Inga's brother's room was made ready for me and Inga spent the night in her old bedroom.

The next morning I awoke early and slipped out of the house before anyone else was up. I walked to the graveyard in the early morning rain, and listened for the voices of the dead. The dead were silent. They had nothing to tell me. I couldn't hear even the rumour of a whisper from them. I could see the tree where Lara had hidden the first time I met her, but there was no ghost of Lara there either. The graveyard I had always imagined as some sort of sanctified space was only a graveyard, and I was filled with sadness. I whistled the

"Ode to Joy," as a kind of defiant gesture, but I was getting soaked from the rain and so I made my way home.

We were married in Winnipeg. The Unitarian minister, Rognvaldur Petursson, conducted the service and it was brief and simple. Johnny stood up for me and Lilja stood up for Inga. The reception was held at the Unitarian church on the corner of Sargent and Sherbrook. It was a modest affair, except that we hired a band that played for people to dance until midnight. Inga's brother and Flora came in by train from Picton. They were in good spirits, and Flora was obviously pregnant and proud of it.

I spoke to Flora at the reception congratulating her on her good fortune.

"My good fortune is much more than you can imagine," she told me. "I realized that I could never live a lie, and so I told Tomas the whole story of my unfortunate life."

"And how did he react?"

"He knew all along. He did not want to bring it up to me and embarrass me."

"How did he know?"

"He is an intelligent man. He went to Winnipeg to investigate and it took him almost no time to piece together my history. But he didn't care because he is in love with me. Isn't that remarkable?"

I agreed that it was remarkable, and asked what this news meant.

"It means that we are coming back here to live," Flora said. "I do not intend to hide from anyone. I have only one life and I intend to live it the best way I can."

The little girls, Maria and Joa, were ecstatic. They could not imagine anything happier than to have more children around. They danced through the whole reception, bumping into the adult dancers and inventing songs to sing to Inga and me. By midnight they were asleep, lying in the benches along the side of the hall, and we carried them home to bed.

Inga began to teach soon after the wedding, but before the year was over she too was on the way to delivering our son, Hannes—named, of course, for my late benefactor. The real estate business in Winnipeg did very well, and Inga soon had to stay home as more children made their way into the world. We had six children in all, and we named the rest of them after Icelandic gods: Thor, Freyja, Nanna, Njord and Frigg. Our children grew up under the shadow of the Great War, but they were not touched by it. By the time the Great Depression hit they were all well educated and secure, and I looked forward to a long life with Inga and many grandchildren. I heard nothing of Lara all those years.

But my long retirement into bliss was not to be. In 1939 Inga died quite suddenly. The doctor said she had a heart attack. At least she didn't suffer. We went to bed happily one night, and when I awoke and put my arm around her I knew that she was gone. I buried her in the graveyard at Gimli, where she rests with the people who had lain on the roofs so many years ago. When I came back to say goodbye to her, I thought I could hear a hundred voices welcoming her.

For five years I lived alone in that house in Winnipeg. My son Hannes had taken over the business and there wasn't much left for me to do. Johnny died young as well, catching the flu in 1918, and Lilja returned to Iceland. I set out to tell my story, and that is the story I have told you. But I am not finished yet.

On August fifteenth, 1945, the day the Second World War ended, I went out into the streets to celebrate with the rest of the people in the city. Nobody stayed home that day. Impromptu parades sprang up. Groups of people gathered and sang. Anybody who could play music was out in the street playing. I couldn't believe there were so many trumpets and bugles and bagpipes in all of Winnipeg. I was tired from all the exuberance, so I found a bench on the Legislative Building grounds, and I sat there imagining what the Golden Boy on top of the Legislative Building might have been thinking.

Then somebody covered my eyes with her hands and said, "Guess who?" I didn't need to guess. That voice was so deeply buried in my mind that I could have recognized it anywhere. "Lara," I called out as if she were a long distance away. "Lara, where have you been?"

"All over the world," she answered. "I've been to Europe and Africa, to Brazil and China, to Australia and to the Northwest Territories."

"Did you marry?" I asked.

"No. My father died and left me enough money that I could do whatever I wished, and so there was no need to get married."

"Have you ever been back here?"

"Yes. I have travelled a lot but I have lived in Winnipeg for most of my life."

"And yet you never talked to me."

"You were married. You brought children into the world. All I could have brought you was unhappiness. But I have had news of you and your doings."

"And now?"

"And now your wife is dead. We have lived long lives and seen many things. Do you still love me?"

"Yes," I said. "That is the same unfortunate situation that I find myself in."

"You remember that I predicted that you would be a sailor and travel the world, and that I would take exotic lovers. It turned out that I was the traveller and you the lover."

"Will you marry me now?"

"I will think about it. I doubt that we need to marry. But we should have one final adventure before our time is up. How is your health?"

"Excellent. Or at least well enough for one of my age."

"Good. Then we will take our trip to the end of the lake. We will take a canoe and travel into the wilderness."

We kissed then to seal the bargain, and the next day we began to plan our trip north to pristine wilderness and to the possibility of other lived lives.

Here the manuscript ends. I have no idea what Lara and my great-grandfather spoke about or the journey they took. My father has no memory of their having travelled down the lake. He says they both ended up in the Betel nursing home in Gimli. Perhaps they did. Or perhaps that's another story. I have done my research and I could find no evidence that they were in Betel. Their gravestones are not in the cemetery at Gimli, so they are not a part of that chorus of voices. I believe they did finally make the trip by canoe up the west side of Lake Winnipeg to Playgreen Lake. But I am a writer and I can believe what I want and make it happen in my writing. I sit in my studio on Lake Winnipeg, right where the first Icelanders landed in New Iceland so long ago, and I imagine their ghosts climbing out of the flatboats on which they travelled and striding up the beach, bringing their meagre possessions to a land about to be ravaged by smallpox. Like my great-grandfather, I go to the cemetery to speak with the dead, and I whistle the "Ode to Joy" for them. They have not complained.

My own story lacks the colour of my ancestors' stories. I was born, as I have told you, with a sense of my own special destiny, and like most people who believe in their destiny, I spent a lot of time waiting for it to arrive. I do remember that I had my own ration book during the war, filled with colourful coupons that my mother clipped to take to the grocery store, and I resented that violation of my property. On my second Christmas, I was given a bright red windup fire chief's toy car, and I was certain then that I would be a fire chief. Later, I saw a Hydro worker with a belt and spurs climb the pole in front of our house and I knew then that I would climb poles for the rest of my life. By the time I went to school, however, I had chosen my vocation. I would be a writer.

In September 1943, a NATO training base came into existence just west of the town, and though the war had seemed distant when it was being fought, the military presence shaped the days of my growing up. When the war ended, the town was flooded with men in uniforms. My father bought a couple of Bren Gun Carriers which he planned to convert into machines that could travel over the snow on the lake in winter. The air was filled with small Harvard trainer planes and later jet aircraft. The searchlight from the airbase swept across the ceiling of the room I shared with my brother every night until I left home.

The air was always filled with airplanes, and we grew accustomed to talking between the roar of the engines. Yellow Harvard training planes and P-51 Mustang fighters were everywhere. Later, they were replaced with CF-100 fighter planes, the only Canadian-designed and produced fighter aircraft ever commissioned.

And with the planes came the pilots being trained, hundreds of young men from NATO: Englishmen, Frenchmen, Swedes, Italians and Turks. We were occupied by the forces of Europe, and that gave Gimli an odd sort of cosmopolitanism. Foreign languages were in the air, and while the rest of Canada had returned to peace, we were always on the brink of war.

My childhood was not extraordinary. I was the oldest of seven children, and that meant that there was little left over either of money or parental doting to give me much sense of my special nature, though I continued to believe that I was a child of destiny. I went to school, walking the two miles to get there every day. The teachers knew of my marathon walk, and they made special allowance for my lateness, which was kind of them, but has since made me a bad guest, always arriving just as the others are prepared to depart.

What is there to say of a childhood, especially a happy one? I played the role of the king in the school play in the first three grades. I sang magnificently off-tune in the choir. I was larger than most of the other boys of my age, so I wasn't bullied. The girls liked me and made me turn the skipping rope for them during recess. The other boys made it clear to me that girls were a different sort of animal, soft but dangerous. And of course I was always falling in love.

The habit of falling in love has stayed with me longer than I had expected it would, and it has propelled me through a string of marriages and relationships that I suppose are typical of the late twentieth century and the beginning of the new millennium, but which don't win you much approval.

Time has seemed to speed up as I age. I remember the advent of rock and roll, Bill Haley and Elvis Presley ushering out the big bands. Like the rest of my generation, I went psychedelic in the sixties. The photos from that era are embarrassing now, because what seemed dangerous and exciting at the time now reads like cliché, a sort of brief costume ball with bell bottoms and beards. I feared the bomb in the fifties, made love not war in the sixties, established a career in the seventies and was seduced by computers in the eighties and nineties. I was always looking forward to something, but I have now reached the stage where the only thing I can look forward to with certainty is death.

And that is perhaps why I have become obsessed with my great-grandfather's journal. I wonder why he stopped writing in it as soon as he was married, then took it up some forty years later. I suppose there was not much to say. He was too old to serve in the Great War, but not by much. In the twenties, he became rich, and my grandfather remembers great balls and parties, but he lost his money in the Depression, or at least he lost his fortune. He lived comfortably, but by 1933 the ball was over. Europe was on the march to fascism and Nazism and communism. And of course I was waiting to be born.

I believe I can remember my great-grandfather Baldur. What my mind gives me is the image of a white-haired man who was tall and elegant, always dressed in a suit and a tie. He wore his suit and tie when he mowed the lawn and when he cranked the old Nash Lafayette to start it. I remember him cranking the generator for the radio, and I remember the fights between Joe Louis and Jersey Joe Walcott, though that may have been my father and his brothers huddled around the radio. They were all Joe Louis fans, and they were all Toronto Maple Leaf fans, so there wasn't much dissension.

Why didn't somebody stop them? Somebody must have known of Baldur and Lara's plans to travel up the lake. They were much too old to undertake such an expedition. Lake Winnipeg is an enormous shallow lake, but it is as dangerous as any body of water in the world. Storms can rise up on a minute's notice, and the shallowness of the lake means that the period of the waves is short, and a boat can be pounded to fragments in minutes. Travelling the lake in a big solid fishing skiff is dangerous. Travelling in a seventeen-foot canoe is madness. But that's what they did. They left on the eighteenth of June in a canoe. They pushed off from the white rock on Willow Island where the first settlers had arrived to create New Iceland, and they were never heard from again.

Or at least they never contacted anyone in the south again. There were fanciful rumours about them, of course. They had built a log cabin in the woods on the shore of Playgreen Lake. They were living with a Native tribe and had adopted Native ways. They had decided to canoe all the way up the Nelson River, through Hudson Bay and so on to Iceland. They had drowned tragically during a storm on the lake. They had returned south but had told no one in Winnipeg and had gone to live in California. They had died from accident or disease, or had simply vanished.

On my sixty-eighth birthday I decided to go and search for them. I knew better than to trust my luck to canoes, and there was my quadruple bypass to consider. I didn't tell you about that, and I won't bore you with the details, but once your heart has been removed from your body and stopped while a machine keeps you alive, you look at things differently. You have been as close to death as you can ever come and still return. The world you return to is not the same as the one you left. It is more luminous, the sun shines more brightly and the way you breathe changes.

I hired a helicopter to fly me out to Norway House at the spot where Lake Winnipeg is drained by the Nelson River. It seemed a quixotic thing to do. Could anyone still alive remember them? It turned out that, yes, quite a few people could remember them, and stories about them had passed on to another generation. I had my recorder with me, and I interviewed everyone I could. Of course the stories about them were not consistent, but many of them remembered a priest named Father Jacob who had been there for several years, and who had known them. "Ask Father Jacob," several people told me, but when I asked where I would find this Father Jacob, no one could help.

There was no trace of Baldur or of Lara in Norway House. I guess I thought that my own passion for the search would turn up some concrete evidence, some traces that would evoke a past that was once a present but which no longer existed. I looked for signs and omens, but there were none. Only the ever-present bush and that highway of a river met me, and they were mute.

I returned in defeat to Winnipeg, but then I received a call from a man who identified himself as Father Jacob. He said that some-one from Norway House had contacted him and told him that I was asking about him. I arranged to meet him at the McNally Robinson bookstore on Grant Avenue.

Father Jacob turned out to be a large, jovial man, bald except for a small fringe, with piercing blue eyes. He had arrived before me, and I assumed since he was the only priest in the restaurant that he was Father Jacob. I greeted him and ordered coffee. He was already drinking a latte.

"You are looking for information about your great-grandfather, I take it?" he said.

"Yes. What can you tell me?"

"Not very much, I'm afraid. I met your great-grandfather and Lara at the end of the war. They were living in a cabin on Playgreen Lake, not far from Norway House. I was a young priest on my first assignment, and I canoed all around the district looking for possible converts. That's how I first found them. They were gracious and invited me in for tea. For a couple of years I dropped by every month or so and listened to stories about early Winnipeg. Then one day, I arrived and there was no one there. The place looked as if they had just stepped out for a few minutes. I waited for about an hour and when they didn't return, I carried on. The next month I returned, and the place was exactly as it had been before. This time I searched the area for clues to their disappearance and found none." He took out a large envelope from a briefcase on the floor near our table. "I did find this," he said and passed me a manuscript. I could tell from the elegant script that it was my great-grandfather's writing.

"I brought this back with me, intending to read it, but I found myself busy and I put it away for another time. Several times I set out to read it, but after a while it seemed a violation to read it, but a burden not to. And now you are here, and I am unburdened."

"What finally happened to them?" I asked.

"I don't know," he answered. "I don't think anyone does know."

We chatted on inconsequently for a few minutes, and then he excused himself. I took the manuscript home, but like Father Jacob, I was loath to begin to read. I waited until evening, then mixed myself a glass of whisky and water and sat down in my chair by the fire and began to read the journal.

BALDUR'S SONG: FINAL CODA

I had intended to begin this journal the very day that Lara had come back into my life, but things have moved far too quickly for that. We had decided to canoe along the west side of the lake until we reached Norway House. We lasted three days. The weather was terrible and the lake was far too rough for a canoe. I began to realize that time had crept up on me a little faster than I had recognized. By the time we reached Gimli and the place of my birth I was so stiff and sore that I could barely walk.

We stayed in Gimli for a week. We went to the graveyard to pay our final respects, but the dead were in no mood for company and they ignored us entirely. The tree behind which Lara had hidden at our first meeting was still there, though it too had suffered the trials of aging. Lightning must have struck it, because the trunk was split in two and the upper branches were dead.

We found a fisherman willing to take us up the lake to Warren's Landing. And from there we could make our way to Norway house House by skiff. I wasn't sure of our final destination, or even if our destination were final. I pored over maps and chose Little Playgreen Lake as the spot where I would build or buy a small cabin.

The headwaters of the Nelson River form an odd amalgamation of lakes and rivers. Playgreen Lake is two lakes joined by a narrow channel. Kiskittogosu Lake and Kisskoto Lake are also attached and a magnificent waterfall leads to Cross Lake. Norway House is on one branch of the Nelson. It was given that name after Lord Selkirk hired a number of Norwegian ex-convicts to build him a series of roads in 1816. In 1817 they built Norway House at Mossy Point to replace the earlier Jack River post.

I had taken Inga to Warren's Landing in 1913, just before the Great War broke out. We spent two nights in the hotel at George's Island and then another ten days at Warren's Landing. The hotel was elegant with wide green lawns where the guests played croquet and held picnics. You had to be careful, because black bears often disturbed the games, though I never heard of a bear attacking a person.

We took the children, Hannes, Thor and Freyja, and they had a wonderful time. I hired a young Cree woman to take care of the children and supervise them while we drank champagne and danced in the summer night. We went out for rides in the fishermen's lovely two-masted sailing skiffs, and explored the beaches where the white pelicans were nesting. We returned on one of the new gas boats that were rapidly replacing the steamboats on the lake.

This, my second journey to the north, was a shock. The hotels had vanished as if they never existed. There were no more manicured lawns. Where there had been a huge fishing enterprise there were now fewer boats and fewer fishermen. Everything seemed wilder and less developed than it had been thirty years earlier.

And yet everything had the scent of new beginnings. The water was clear and the spruce and tamarack were a green that I remembered but hadn't seen for years. Birds were everywhere and the symphony of their songs made the forest alive.

We arrived on a gas boat late one afternoon near the end of

August. The fisherman who had brought us was reluctant just to drop us off on a sandy beach with no sign of any habitation, but we insisted we would be fine. He took us ashore on a small lifeboat, and made another trip to bring our supplies. Then we watched as he left us and his boat disappeared around a point of land. We were alone at last.

"Well, here we are," Lara said. "This is the spot to which our lives have taken us."

"It's a good spot," I told her. "A good spot for an ending."

"Or for a beginning," she said, "though who can tell the difference between endings and beginnings?"

"Do we have any plan?" I asked. "Any hopes or desires, and sense of a future?"

"No. We will see what happens. But we are still alive and we have to take measures to ensure that we continue to stay alive. I am not here to commit suicide."

"Nor I. Although I have wondered over the past few days whether we weren't doing precisely that."

"Set up the tent," she said. "Build a fire. I will find us some food."

I set up the tent and lit a fire. Lara cooked eggs and bacon over the open fire, a fine breakfast, though it was early evening. We ate silently, and watched the fire burn. The sun set in the west, though some trick of the imagination made it seem to me that it was setting in the north.

"What's that?" Lara asked, pointing out over the lake. At first I saw nothing, but after a minute I made out a large canoe skirting the shore. There were several figures in the canoe, and I had a moment's fear that they might be hostile. We watched until it crunched onto the shore right where we were camped.

A man scrambled out and asked, "Are you all right?"

"Yes," I answered. "Won't you join us for a cup of tea?"

The other two people in the canoe got out and they all came over to where we were sitting in front of the fire. There was a man who introduced himself as Monkman and a woman and a girl. The woman's name was Edith and the girl was Tanya. We introduced our-selves and Lara poured them each a cup of tea.

"You don't have a boat," Monkman pointed out.

"No," I said. "Not yet. But perhaps you can help us to buy one."

"What kind of boat do you want?"

"I want a skiff and a canoe."

"I can sell you this canoe. And my brother has a skiff he will sell."

"Good. And we are also looking for a cabin on Playgreen Lake."

"Little Playgreen?"

"Yes."

"There are several there. You can use one of them."

"Doesn't someone own them?"

"Never heard of anyone owning them. Whoever wants to use them uses them. They need a quite a lot of work if you are going to spend more than a couple of nights."

We drank our tea, and Monkman said he would come out with the skiff for us the next day. Lara had spoken with the women while I was dealing with Monkman. She told me that Tanya was small but she was not a young girl. She had been a nurse with the army, and had just arrived here herself. She was on her way to Norway House to work there.

"Is she Métis?" I asked.

"No. But I don't know what she is."

We sat at the fire, not talking but watching the embers rise up in a wind that had just started. The sparks moved over the lake like fireflies, and then drowned in the water. I told Lara once more that I loved her, and she nodded yes, I know. Then we climbed into our sleeping bags and I fell instantly into a deep and dreamless sleep.

The next morning Monkman was there bright and early as he had promised. He was driving a small skiff with an outboard motor and towing his canoe behind. We loaded our supplies into the skiff and Monkman took us for a ride of about eight or ten miles to Little

Playgreen Lake. We stopped at a cabin made from logs chinked with clay. It was on a small rise about a hundred feet from the shore.

"This is the best cabin out here," he said. "But don't plan on wintering in it unless you can chop a couple of cords of wood. There's no insulation and the winds out here can be really wicked."

I thanked him and asked what it would cost for the skiff and the canoe. We settled on four hundred dollars, which I thought was a fair price. He left then but told me that he'd be back with the canoe the following morning.

Lara and I spent the morning cleaning up the cabin and storing our supplies. I fished for about an hour and caught two pickerel and a couple of small perch. I had brought a double-barrelled shotgun, and I bagged a spruce grouse just back behind the cabin. It looked as if finding food was not going to be as difficult a task as I had imagined.

And thus began two of the happiest years of my life. I sent for materials and insulated the cabin. We received regular shipments of supplies from the south via the post at Norway House. We were up early in the mornings and we walked the forest paths. In the winter we huddled in our little cabin and warmed ourselves by the fire. We met the Native people, though their lives were very different from our own. The local priest, Father Jacob, visited us often and brought news from the wide world, though that other world seemed far away and unlikely to touch us.

Then, one day in late summer of our second year, things began to change. Lara seemed quieter than I remembered. She had always had a sense of play and a willingness to go beyond what others would regard as seemly or correct. Now, she was thoughtful and introspective. I tried to talk to her about our youth, but she didn't enter the conversation as I hoped she would. I had been out hunting, and I brought a grouse back to the cabin where Lara was sitting on a chair at the table, looking out the window toward the lake. At first I thought she was asleep, but she stood up and beckoned me to come to the window. She pointed in the direction of the sun that was just setting.

"It's perfect," she said. "Absolutely perfect."

"Yes," I answered. "It seems timeless. I took her in my arms and we stood motionless for several minutes. The sun dropped below the horizon and the sky to the west turned to a stunning panorama of blues and reds and greens. Finally, dusk settled in and we sat there in the darkness.

The next afternoon Lara walked to the shore and waded knee-deep into the lake. It felt like silence but the cries of the gulls and the splashing of the terns were the lead instruments in the birdsong that was everywhere. I sat on the sand and watched her wading. A big white pelican landed in the water only a few feet away.

"This would be a perfect time for the world to end," Lara told me when she joined me on the shore.

"It will end soon enough," I said.

"Yes. It will end sooner for me than for others. I am sick, Baldur, and I feel my death growing in me. I grow weaker daily. I will be happy for these days, but I know that an ending is near."

I tried to reassure her, but she did not wish to be reassured. "I am not a child," she said. "I know what is inevitable and I have probably known it for longer than I could admit even to myself. We were innocent children when we first met. I hope to die with the same innocence."

She had not seen any doctor. No one had diagnosed her with any illness. She had conjured her own death without help. And I believed her. She knew something she couldn't name. I held her in my arms for a long time, and we looked over the water. The universe was indifferent to our state. The birds continued to bicker and the breeze from the north hinted at the coming of winter, though we were perfectly warm.

"I want to travel back in the direction of New Iceland," I told her. "I don't want to get there, but I want to aim toward the people of the smallpox who are still whispering in the graveyard." I had formulated a plan in that moment. We would wait for another month, then paddle down along the west shore of the lake to the Narrows where the lake formed an hourglass, and every storm was magnified by the current that rushed between the north basin and the south. We would set up a camp there and wait for a storm. Then we would bind ourselves together, enter the canoe and launch ourselves into whatever awaited us after this world.

Lara thought there was no reason why I should follow her, but my mind was made up. Is made up. This is my last entry in this journal. I await whatever will happen.

And thus ends my great-grandfather's journal. I sat for several hours contemplating his story, and then I went to bed. The following day I drove out to Gimli and the New Iceland cemetery. The place has been renewed. There is no bush, only stately old spruce trees. The lawn is carefully tended. A cenotaph contains the names of those who are buried there. I searched the names, and recognized many of them. I whistled as best I could the "Ode to Joy," and asked for guidance, but there was no response. They who lie there are now content with their state, and have no need to speak to the living.

That night I sat by my fireplace and reread the journal from start to finish. I imagined Baldur and Lara spending their last days in a sort of trance, happy to be alive and in love, moving through their days with slow deliberation, preparing for an ending of their own making. I traced in my mind their slow progress south to the Narrows along the granite cliffs and outcroppings. I visualized them camping on the shore in a tent, waiting while the sun rose and set on perfect weather.

Then finally a storm arises, a wind from the northwest and

blinding rain. They dress carefully, bind themselves together and get into the canoe. A couple of strokes of the paddle and they are into the heart of the storm. The canoe is steady, but it bucks and spins in the surging rapids. They kiss, and then are lost, spun out of history into myth, out of the reach of love and of smallpox, drawn through the river into a sort of rebirth I cannot imagine.

Perhaps they have entered a new world, like the New Iceland into which they were born. Perhaps our whole family will follow them into wherever they have gone. I believe they will be waiting, there at the end of time. There will be music then, the "Ode to Joy," Baldur's song.